The Perfect Imperfections of My Life

Vedanti Khanna

Invincible Publishers

First published in India in 2019

ISBN : 978-93-88333-43-6

Invincible Publishers

201A, SAS Tower, Sector 38, Gurgaon-122003

Registered Address: Opposite Kasturba Ashram, Radaur, Haryana–135133

Printed at Thomson Press (India) LTD

"One of the basic rules of universe is that nothing is perfect.
Perfection simply doesn't exist...

Without imperfection, neither you nor I would exist."

- Stephen Hawking

Acknowledgements

My sincere thanks to the brilliant people who have worked behind the scenes to make *The Perfect Imperfections of My Life* happen.

Enormous thanks to my parents for believing in me to an extent that no parent could ever believe in their child. I am pretty sure without them I would have never found the world to which I actually belonged, the world of writing. Thanks to my little brother Atharva and Grandparents for never failing to motivate me.

I am deeply indebted to Anika Chhabra, the girl behind the character of Brooklyn Hart. Girl, you motivated me at a point when I wasn't sure if I could or I should continue writing this novel. Big thanks to Ananya Srivastava for being the first listener of my story and for encouraging me to turn it into a novel. Thank you Utkarsh Sharma, Tanishq Srivastava, and Parth Kumra for helping me out with the research work. Thanks to all my friends, cousins and family for being even more excited than me throughout this journey and motivating me at every point.

Most importantly I want to thank my Granddad for patiently reading and editing my novel every evening and saving me from all the clangers. I learnt so much from him.

Finally, thanks to my publishers, the Invincible team for realising my potential and helping me tell this story to the world.

And now, after living the lives of Aarika, Ayan, Samar, Kevin, Brooklyn and Flynn for 738 days, I am Vedanti again!

Table of Content

Prologue

"And when I found you, for the first time in my life I felt that I was happy, satisfied. I was always bored but never of you." He says running his fingers through my uncombed hair and slowly running the knife up and down my body that has a dead person's smell all over it, making it much scarier than it already is. "But, do you know which day was even better? When I saw you transforming into a lunatic, begging to your so-called God for your sanity, right in front of my eyes. I had never been more entertained in my life." He is roaring with laughter and has the same twinkle in his eyes that a lion has when he finally finds his prey. More than his knife, the fact that hurts me is, how could he do this to the love of his life? A few days back I was the love of his life. His friend. And what hurts me more is that the love I respected so much never existed.

"You were so, so beautiful, my God, I can't even tell. Specially your heart, that I couldn't resist to tear it down into a hundred pieces. I mean that in a literal way, by the way. You were irresistible, so irresistible to hurt, to torture, to play with. So perfectly charming that I wanted to rip your soul off, into a thousand pieces. But now I just want to crack your lovely skull and pity the wretched and superfluous thoughts inside it, which can never be compared to mine." His laughter grows louder and louder as he says each word and pushes the dead body closer to my feet.

"Please let me go!" I beg of him. I can barely speak. I never knew a day would come when I'd have to make this much effort to even speak.

"Sir, you are under arrest." I take a breath of relief as the cops break into the room with handcuffs and guns in their hands.

***

Have you ever wondered where our destiny can take us? It is destiny that makes us fall in a pit and it is the same destiny that helps us to get out. The world, as we call it, 'modern', is not modern but is actually becoming foolish. We live to please others and not ourselves. I did that too until an imperfection came to my life that without my realization actually made it perfect. We live life as a race in which we only want to go the fastest, and not as a journey. We run without admiring the simple pleasures that come in the way. We all want our lives to be perfect, but if perfection is our destination, then we all need a train to reach there, which not only halts at stations of joy, progress, and enjoyment, but also those of pain, heartbreaks, disappointment, and fraud. The train will halt at numerous stations, but ultimately it will take you to your desired destination. Even I took a lot of time to realise this, but once I understood it, my life changed. I understood this even better when life taught me really unexpected and unwanted lessons that helped me reach where I am today. This story began when I was fourteen, so let me start from the beginning. Welcome to my bittersweet journey.

2005
Trust me not

"Going to miss you so much!" Standing on the top of my favourite hill, I yelled on the top of my voice with my backpack on my back, camera hanging in the neck, and my eyes full of tears. Feeling the cold breeze trying to calm the burning fire in my heart, I reminisced all the beautiful moments I had spent there, and captured that beautiful view in my camera. It was hard, so hard to leave the place where I had lived for fourteen long years! I couldn't believe that these are my last few hours in Mussoorie. I remember whenever I used to be angry at anyone, that hill used to be my escape place. It felt that it was better to jump from that hill right into that valley with those colourful butterflies and flowers, rather than leaving it for the hot, humid beaches of Mumbai.

But I am just fourteen, so I am no one to have a say in such big decisions of life. After all, dad has worked day and night to build a palace like mansion for all of us in Mumbai. I have barely seen my dad in the past two years. It is unimaginable how hard it must have been for mom to live without him all this while. He used to come and before any of us felt contented, he was gone. But now, all of that is going to be over. We all were going to live together. Yet I did not want to leave this heavenly place, it was just so hard.

My grandma held my fingers in her hand and tied my hair like she used to when I was six. But she pulled back and tried to hide her face as she was barely able to hold her tears. I knew out of all of us, she was the most heartbroken as she always used to tell me that her life without me is unimaginable. She thinks I am beautifully special. We would play games like crossword, read and discuss the verses of Bible, talk about even the silliest of things. She is really cool for her age and perhaps even a teenager couldn't understand other teenagers as precisely she does. She is the one I could confide in, or to be more precise she was my human diary. It just made me want to shout so loudly on mom, dad, everyone that *Why on earth are you doing something which is hurting everyone like thorns in their hearts?*

Granddad and grandma bid us a farewell and we boarded the plane. Soon the view of the hills changed to that of the plains, and I knew so will my life. I listened to some songs; watched other passengers having gleaming smiles on their faces. Even Mom and Kevin are more than thrilled to leave everything back and begin a new life. It was only me waiting for the plane to take the wrong way and land back in Dehradun. I couldn't help but have a hope in my heart that everything will be fine, a hope that I'll be happy, a hope that I'll meet amazing people there. Hope is the only thing I had.

***

From isolating myself from the rest of the family for weeks so that I can convey my annoyance, to lying on the floor and crying like ten-year-old, I did everything to stop this change of cities. But guess what, these efforts were futile and thus, here I landed in the city of dreams — Mumbai. It was my first day in school. Unlike my school in Mussoorie, this one is fully air-conditioned with a highly sophisticated architectural design having a playground four times the size of my previous school. As I entered the classroom there was silence and a strange expression on everyone's face. I was baffled before everyone broke into a loud laughter. I broke out into a cold sweat.

"Guys, this is Aarika Martins, your new classmate. I hope you'll not let her feel out of place and guide her. I expect you all not to treat her the same way as you have treated all the new students until now. Don't you dare bother her. Aarika, I'll be back in a minute, please take a seat." It was Miss Sarah, the class teacher who introduced me. Unlike the students, she seemed quite sweet. I was surprised to see that she had such a friendly relation with the children.

"What are you doing, Aarika Martins? Don't you know Alisha is going to sit here? Go away." A guy said as if some queen named Alisha is going to kill him if he lets anyone else sit on that chair, as if it was gilded. "You, don't you sit here, Tia and her boyfriend are going to sit here." A girl talked to me as if I, some maid, had entered a kingdom I wasn't supposed to. God, where was I? Just changing towns felt as if I have moved to another planet. I didn't ever experience these things in my school in Mussoorie.

"You surely don't want to sit here. His hair smelt really bad. Why do you put so much oil on your head, boy? Eww." Another voice came from behind. "Do you seriously think an aunty like her would mind that?" A guy started laughing. My God has always taught me to never judge anyone, but that doesn't mean I would keep quiet if someone else judges me. "Who are you to point a speck of sawdust in my eye when you yourself have a plank in your eye? My Lord says that judging is one of the greatest sins so beware of what you are doing."

Everyone's reaction was the last reaction I ever expected. They were laughing so loudly that some of them even had tears in their eyes. "Sawdust? Lord? Sorry, but I think you've mistaken this school to be a church!" a guy said, trying hard to control his laughter. I was too nervous to look at anyone now. I quietly went and take the corner most seat. Neither anyone tried to interact with me, nor did I. Not that I have an attitude like them but I was just shy, too shy to get even a single word out of my mouth. I heard whispers coming from all around. There was only one thing common, I heard the word 'aunty' in all of them.

The day was awful, I got into trouble for the most random things. As soon as the bell for the last period rang, I collected my things and rushed to hide in some corner. But struck by someone's foot, I had a great fall, causing my specs to fly to the other side. While I searched for my specs and made efforts to get up, I already saw people quickly clicking pictures and then running before I got to say anything. Such freaks these people are.

***

I realized that grandma was right. I am special. But definitely not the way she used to think. I haven't stood in front of the mirror for this long ever. To go down the memory lane, fifteen minutes would have been my highest record. But today I have been standing for three long hours, trying to figure out and look at my flaws like the people in my posh school do. I agree I am a bit too skinny. But nobody is perfect. My long, thick braid isn't like their funky hairstyles other girls have, but I love it. People have always had the preconception about girls being over concerned about their looks and appearance. But I have always believed in simplicity. Rather than utilizing my energy in enhancing my beauty, I have preferred to use it in more important things. Comfort, comfort is the thing I look for. My looks, my clothes, my hairstyle and all such similar things never mattered to anyone in Mussoorie. But now it seems as if these are the only important things.

***

When I came back after having a shower, I experienced some new feelings. Sometimes I heard some voices from the house adjacent to mine. This time I heard a beautiful melody coming. It wasn't any song that I was aware of, before but I think that boy had composed it himself.

I sat along the wall and gently closed my eyes and felt each word bring my burdened veins to peace. As he strummed the strings of the guitar, my heart too started singing along. Dancing barefoot in the dark, with happiness in my arms, oh how marvellous it was that night! It was like within a few seconds I was taken to a completely different world, where no worries, no desolation existed. Goosebumps appeared on my arms, my heart was dancing and laughing again. I never knew any such feeling existed. I never knew that there was magic in music. I never knew that it would take only this much for my worries, my sadness to go away.

***

Days and days had gone by and slowly his singing had become that part of my day which I really looked forward to. When surrounded by his beautiful ditties, it was as if nothing else really mattered. I was so charmed by the songs that I wanted to praise that guy in person. I even tried peeping into his house several times but never managed to see him. I never actually stepped out of the house, so there wasn't any chance of seeing him anyway.

***

It's been three months and things at the school haven't been any better. Seeing people do graffiti on my locker, throwing balls of paper with weird comments written on it in between the classes, is now not any unfamiliar sight for me. My life's turned upside down. Everything was so simple back there in Mussoorie. No late-night parties, no fashion, no hustle and bustle! Mom and Kevin didn't take much time to fit in. Dad's happiness knows no bounds to have all of us here. But it's better if no one asks what difficulties I am facing. This loud music at the parties to which I am forcibly taken, makes me deaf. The glittering gowns and faces mock my simplicity. I don't belong in here. I don't want to. How fake their lives are! I can't even breathe here like I wish to. It all suffocates me so much. Their fake smiles, their fake happiness, it all haunts me. Will this elite society ever accept a person like me?

But there's one place in the whole school that makes me escape this ugly world of reality ,which feels like my perfectly fantasized world—my school's music room. I often go there in the break time when it is usually isolated. I work on improving my vocals and sometimes play the violin too. I am not very familiar with the instrument as when I started taking lessons, soon after we had to leave for Mumbai. That was another reason I did not want to come here. But two days back something embarrassing happened. I was in another world when the sound of claps brought me back. Those pair of chuck hazel gleaming eyes were admiring me, that charming smile was full of appreciation, those silky, soft black hair, that face even fairer than mine, every part of him was looking at me with surprise.

"Beautiful voice. But that's not how you play it." The guy took away the violin from my hands, scoffed, and started playing and singing along. His voice sent vibrations all over my body and my heart was elated all of a sudden until I realized that he was the same guy I had adored for days now.

"Sorry, I got to leave. Catch you later." I didn't have guts to face him. I was all freaked out. How could he come in front of me out of nowhere? This isn't the kind of encounter I had hoped for.

"Hey dorkhead, still no friends huh? Anyway, I am not surprised. You know what, you should publish a book—101 ways to be a total freak! I assure you it's going to be a bestseller!" While I was sitting in the cafeteria and having lunch, Alisha came and hit me on the back of my head unreasonably, and then walked past me so easily. I heard various people laughing from behind. It had become intolerable for me. Just because I am patient, it doesn't mean I don't have any self-respect.

"Yeah that's true I don't have any friends, maybe because I am not a coquette like you. Oh, and how can I forget to mention, a fake person as well?" I just could not believe I said that. Oh God please forgive me! But she deserved it. If they accept it or not, but everyone was trying really hard not to laugh.

"Sorry, what exactly did you say?" Alisha came very close to my face, with her bloodshot eyes and started hurting my foot with hers. I grabbed the cup of cold coffee from the table and threw it on her plastic, ugly face. There was a sudden hubbub of laughter and shouting. While there were some who came immediately and started asking her if she's okay and wiping the coffee off her face. Alisha had gone all wild and mad now. She was roaring with anger. She was clawing at my face and latching on to my hair just like a wild beast. She had overpowered me. She was hauntingly strong. For a minute, I felt as if I was going to return home with absolutely no hair today until someone came.

"Back off Alisha! Stop it right now!" He was the same guy I met in the music room.

"Not today Ayan. Not after what she has done," she said pulling my hair even harder.

"Last chance Alisha," that guy said again.

"Okay, fine Ayan. If you say so. I see you haven't gotten over your ability of supporting wrong people." I was shocked that a person like her even listened to someone.

"And I see you still haven't gotten over your lunacy?" that guy said so calmly as if Alisha was his puppet or something.

"You bitch, I am going to ruin you. You are so very close to destruction now." she whispered in my ear as she left the cafeteria.

"I think you are a really busy girl and not even courteous enough to listen to what the other person has got to say. To be honest, I think Alisha is right in calling you a freak. So, if you can ever spare time from your important business or whatever you do, let me know if you'd like to join the school band. That's what I wanted to ask you in the music room."

"Sorry, but that's the meanest, rudest, and the most impertinent way of talking I have come across. And yes, I would like to be a part of the band. Also, thank you for all your help out there, but in future I would never want someone like you to help me. Have a good day. It was surprising that my apprehensions about someone could change so drastically within seconds. I adored that guy so much a night before and now I never wanted to see him again. Well that's not possible because I was joining the band, but I won't let his presence affect me.

"Tomorrow, music room at 10, sharp. A minute late and you'll be out." Oh God, he was driving me crazy. Does impudence run in everyone's blood here?

"Unfortunately, you'll never get a chance to chuck me out as I know very well the value of time." I made the ugliest face I could and walked away.

***

When I reached the music room, I saw no one else but him. I felt as if all the brow beatings and silly warnings were just for me. He looked at me, but didn't even care to acknowledge my presence and continued with setting the instruments in place.

"Hello, good morning," breaking the silence, I wished him. But he just nodded in response. I agree I wished very rudely, but at least I had the manners to greet. It seemed he lacked even that.

"I would really like to know, what exactly would it cost you to be nice to someone. For once at least."

"I don't intend to have any meaningless conversations and waste my time. Unless you've got something important to say, stop chattering and start practicing." He was truly unbelievably insolent. Other band members soon joined us and much to my surprise they are so much better and lively as compared to the people in this school I have interacted with until now.

***

After school we went to Inayat's place for practicing after two hours of argument. Her place was the best suited as her parents wouldn't be back before twelve in the night but she wouldn't just agree to that. She's a cleanliness freak and was pretty sure we'd make a mess in her big mansion. She is a snobby rich kid, but in the end was kind enough to let us practice at her place. We had to extend the practice as soon there would be a school trip and most of the band members are interested in going.

It had just been eight hours that we had been together but from what I'd heard and witnessed myself, I have got to know a lot about our members. Neil, the pianist is the comedian of the group. He may not have been born with a perfect sense of humour, but his clumsiness alone is enough to arouse everyone's laughter. He keeps bumping into things and absent-mindedly makes jokes on himself. We all can't help but laugh at what a gawk he is. And the other one is Arman, the drummer. I don't know what these people would have done without him. He brings the most delectable food one can find in Mumbai. Inayat's the cellist. She doesn't talk very nicely to anyone and especially to me. Maybe my styles are a little too substandard for a posh girl like her. Then there's Eddy. I seriously haven't been able to figure out much about him, but he's an outstanding rapper. The other one. Oh, I just can't stand him. It's Ayan. There's nothing much to him apart from the fact that he is the male vocalist, fiddler, virtuoso, and the leader of the band. And then there's me, the female vocalist and a lost and troubled soul, seeking her shelter in a strange school in this cool yet weird band.

***

Neil, Arman, and Eddy had already left and I'd begun to feel a little out of place. Ayan was busy working on the finer details of the song, but my part was left untouched. It came out to be amazing and unexpectedly even Ayan commended me for that. Inayat had already changed into her night dress and wasn't doing much apart from making lame jokes on me that no one was finding funny, and also continuously trying to attract Ayan's attention towards her. She was just another chic in Alisha's group. What else was expected of her?

***

"How are you going to get home?" Ayan asked packing his things.

"I have been calling my parents for so long now, but none of them are taking my calls. They are probably in a meeting or something. So, I guess I am just going to sit in the park and wait."

"I thought you were sensible enough to ask one of us to drop you on our way back. But each time your foolishness mocks my faith in you" he jeered at me.

"Look, just do me a simple favour and leave me alone. I am sick of your cheeky and lame comments. They aren't even funny anymore. Just go." I signalled him with my hands.

"Tell me your address now, I am calling the driver." My self esteem was telling me not to go with him but my curiosity was telling me to give him the address and see the fun of it when he found that I live next door to him. I went with my curiosity.

"What the f...? Yours is the family that just shifted! Oh God I can't believe it your shadow is all around me." The colour of his face faded.

"Oh, dear boy, even I am not proud of this very fact. Wish I could help it," I said with even a sadder voice.

"Stop chattering now and start walking," he said, taking my bag away from me.

"But you said you were calling your driver and give me my bag back!" I snatched it from him. He walked so fast that I almost had to run after him to catch up.

"Look at her. You don't know how guilty she must feel for not using her feet to the fullest when she had it. You never know the value of anything until you lose it. Anyway, our houses are not very far away from here. And as far as that bag is concerned, you look like you will die under the burden of that heavy bag or may as well be blown away with the wind. So, I was just trying to help." He said pointing at an old lady on a wheelchair and taking my bag again.

"You'd be the last person I would want help from." I snatched my bag again, almost hurting his hand this time. I am never this mean, rude girl but he's earned it himself.

"Just be quiet and keep walking." He scolded me as if he was my dad or something.

"It's not like I am dying to talk to you. You seriously don't have to do me any favour."

"Okay then I was planning to stop by my aunt's for a little while as my mom has to work late today, then go to the market and purchase a new pick for my guitar. All of that is going to make me hungry so I may as well stop for dinner. Good bye Martins. Hope to see you tomorrow. Alive. Beware of the pickpockets and the murderers." He started walking in the opposite direction. Oh God, I could not go all alone. The weather too looked so scary. It would have started raining any moment.

"I am sorry. I won't speak now, I promise." With my fists clenched, eyes on the ground, only I know what it took me to get these words out of my mouth. He was the last person I wanted to apologize to. But at that moment this was the only choice I had.

"Good for you." He tried hard not to chuckle.

The distance from Inayat's house to our place is not as less as Ayan said. If it was on me, I wouldn't have preferred walking this much ever, but Sir Ayan has his own, crazy theories. Also, I am fond of long walks but with a good company. There was just an awkward long silence between us, just an exchange of mocking comments in between. I am not used to being so quiet.

Soon, the wind started blowing fiercely, so much that my glasses fell off my face. I couldn't help but laugh at myself for so long and Ayan just looked at me as if I was a lunatic straight out of a mental asylum. The biting cold rain drops started falling and I just couldn't control my urge to sing. Without caring what people might think of me I started singing. And also, apart from Ayan there was hardly anyone around me. Being judged by him was not going to have the slightest effect on me. So, unashamedly and unapologetically I started singing and relishing every drop, every beat of rain. It felt after a long, long time as if I was woven into blankets and cloaks of joy.

"Whoa Martins! You are something else." He smiled a little, for the first time. Oh lord this was a miracle.

"Yeah I am an artistic piece of shit."

"You are funny" he said.

"And you are mean" I giggled.

"Compliment right back at you. Be on time tomorrow, bye."

"Want to join for dinner?" I asked, just in order to return his favour and also keeping in mind the fact that his mom wasn't at home.

"In your dreams," he gave a lopsided smile.

"Oh, how could I forget that being nice for more than a minute causes physical agony to you."

"I was just kidding, dinner's already ready. Go home now. Bye."

***

We assembled again after school, but this time at Neil's house as no one wanted to hear Inayat's incessant lamenting over what a mess we had made of her beautiful room.

Neil did something funny again and everyone was laughing their hearts out, but Ayan was just giving his same hesitant smile. I did not like it. I wanted him to join in our enjoyment. Silently I went next to him and tickled on his neck.

"Have you gone mad, Martins?" He broke out into a wild laughter.

"See, it's not that you don't know how to laugh. You have got, um, if not gorgeous, then at least an okay laugh. In fact, it gives one comfort from your intense, mysterious looks. Why are you ashamed of laughing? Cherishing these moments? This life is yours, you haven't stolen it from anyone." I said, tickling him harder this time.

"Whoa! Whoa! Whoa! What is going on here? Arman, don't you think they both are so cute together?" Neil said smirking at Ayan and me. I have got to admit. It was one of the most embarrassing moments of my life. If Alisha would hear this, she'd probably die laughing.

"Bro, even I see some love blooming here," Arman said with his eyes wide open.

"Stop this nonsense, we are running out of time, back to work everyone." Ayan was equally embarrassed.

***

It was a satisfying practice today. I felt really happy of how better my singing had become even though it was a result of Ayan's assistance. That boy never took any classes, nobody taught him at home, but still sings like an angel. Such people are what we call 'gifted'.

"It's Christmas eve today, I want to stop somewhere on our way back home." I said checking my bag to make sure that I had kept the things.

"Where?" he asked, keeping his violin back in the cover.

"Just keep following me."

"Aarika, why the hell have you brought me to an orphanage? Sorry, I do not have time for this."

"What do you have to do? Get home and gorge yourself on another large pizza? Come on wear this cap." I handed Ayan a Santa cap and I wore one too.

"I cannot believe you are making me do this," He said wearing the cap.

Going to places like these is always a terrific experience. They make you value the small little things in your life that you otherwise take for granted. They tell you that happiness is present in each and every speck of life. Despite all the deprivation, all the problems, you can still find happiness if you try. I distributed chocolates among the orphans and also some stationery.

"Will you play it for us?" A cute little boy of about seven years asked Ayan, pointing at his violin.

"We are getting late right now, friend. I promise we are going to come back again and that too very soon." I half- heartedly told him as I didn't want him to get hurt because I know Ayan would never play for them and say something mean in return.

"No Aarika, you can spare at least five minutes out of your busy schedule." Without giving it a second thought, Ayan started playing his violin. It's a true treat for the melody-deprived ears. The kids were so exuberant and joyous that they started dancing. Their eyes were gleaming with delight.

***

Ayan tried to hide it, but I could see that his eyes were wet. He was upset and happy at the same time.

"I cannot tell you Martins how guilty I feel. I became so bitter after my dad's death. I felt guilty for laughing or enjoying anything without him. And that has made me so, so bitter. I was not the same person two years back. And today, I feel even guiltier after looking at these kids. They neither have their mom nor their dad, yet they are dealing with it so cheerfully." He could not control anymore and was drenched in a pool of tears.

"Look Ayan, I can't even feel half the pain that you or those kids go through every day, but I know one thing that if your father had been alive today, he would've wanted you to be happy. He'd want you to cherish your life which he couldn't. Being sad will not make you bring anyone who's already gone. So just live, live your life."

"Whoa, despite all her lunacy, Martins does know how to give a piece of advice. Thank you for taking me there. I have never felt so contented in my life. Playing for them was the best thing I've ever done."

"I know, nothing can make you as happy as doing something for others. It is the best, best feeling ever."

“That’s too much philosophy for me to handle in a single day.” I could see his unhesitant, wide smile for the first time in so many days. I won’t lie, it was charming.

***

It’s been fifteen days since we’ve been practicing and I can’t believe what an amazing piece six minds and hearts have been able to produce. It is just marvellous. I do have a strong feeling that we are going to win. My days in the school are horrible, but band practices are awesome. Also, I have come to the conclusion that Ayan isn’t as bad as I thought.

An official announcement was made for the much-awaited school trip to Nainital. Alisha’s terror has given everyone another reason to trouble me. I had been welcomed to this school in such a way that even if someone comes to talk to me, I know it that they are up to something to trouble me. Such a good welcome in the school was enough to make me aware that the travelling company wouldn’t be good. Ayan and Neil weren’t going. Inayat and Arman had their own friend circle and none of them would want me in their groups. So, even I thought of backing out.

“Honey, I think you should definitely go. Go make some friends. How long will you keep moaning about what is gone? What is gone is gone now, and it cannot come back. Move on now. You cannot find a better opportunity than this trip to do so.” I thought maybe what mom was saying is right. I thought I needed to explore. I needed to make new friends. I couldn’t be a loner always.

***

The whistle blew and the train started moving. I took the window seat, with no one by my side and watched mom and dad waving me a goodbye. Almost all the parents had left, but they were looking and waving at me as if I am stepping out of the house for the first time. Everyone in the train soon became so busy that my presence was unnoticed. They did glance at me, but with mocking eyes, probably thinking why I am here, because trips are something people go to for enjoyment with their friends. And not a shadow of a person was seen around me.

"Hey Aarika, I didn't get a chance to apologize for whatever happened that day. But I have realized my mistake and I want to say, I am really, really sorry. You will forgive me, won't you?" Alisha said, coming and sitting beside me. Forgiveness is a divine virtue. That's what I have always been taught. Of course, I forgave her.

"I am sorry too for what all I did. I shouldn't have said those things." I said putting as calm and sweet demeanour as possible.

"Oh, you are such a darling Aarika, isn't she guys? Come join us. It's going to be so much fun. And what's up with those glasses? Ah, and trust me that braid doesn't look too good." She said removing my glasses and untying my braid. Her group insisted a lot so I joined them. I did have a marvellous time with them, laughing and singing, but it was way too much for me to digest that 'cool' people like them would ever want me in their group, and someone like Alisha could be as sweet as sugar.

We reached Nainital at around 8 in the night. All the memories of Mussoorie once again came to life by being among the hills and chilly weather in Nainital. I was sharing the room with three other girls; Alisha, Veronica, and Tia. While everyone was still dancing, I decided to sleep as I was having a severe headache. I was so deep in sleep that I didn't even hear the door opening, but I was not that deep in sleep that I could not feel those pair of hands tying the cloth around my mouth and other pair of hands covering my eyes. My hands fought hard to reach for the spectacles lying on the table but they were quick enough to throw me into a dark, stinking, spooky room, full of spider webs and rats, and then locked it.

Thrown, just thrown like I am not a human being but just a piece of useless garbage dump. So cold, so helpless, crying I sat between those rats. Wondering who could do something like this.

The touch of those rats on my skin, screams—those suffocating beads of perspiration were all that surrounded me. The door opened after a few hours but whoever opened it was fast enough to run. I somehow reached back.

After returning, all I wanted was revenge from those people and to blurt out everything to a friend. I saw everyone, Alisha, Tia, Veronica, Rihan, and Aman sitting on the breakfast table. I just wanted to go and share everything with them. Trying to wipe away my tears I ran towards their table but overheard something soon that stopped me from going any further. They were so busy laughing at the video that they didn't even notice me standing right behind them. I could hear myself crying in the video and their voices whispering things like, "Hey see there, Aarika Martins totally freaking out! I pity those rats that they are in a company of such an aunty. Wait, is she trying to dance? What an aunty! Oh, we can't even look at her anymore. Bloody aunty!" I couldn't believe they did something like this to laugh around with everyone else later? For a revenge for such a small thing? They had edited the video and added weird sounds. I thought them to be my friends. Let alone friends, they are not even worthy of being called humans. I was just shattered.

"What do you guys think? You'll be saved? I am going to complain to the principal!" I banged their table and looked at them with my red eyes.

"Aww honey, so innocent you are. If you do that then be ready to face the music. Be ready for the snakes next time, if you know what I mean. Argh you stink," laughing, Rihan whispered in my ear. "I told you that I was going to ruin you," Alisha said with the most devilish and ugliest smile. After hearing what they said, I felt that it was better to be quiet and forget the whole thing rather than fighting with these goons.

When I got back home, I didn't mention the incident to anyone as mom and dad were already having business issues, and my brother Kevin had no time for me as he was busy enjoying his college life to the fullest. It had been three days and those memories just won't stop haunting me. Each night I lay down to sleep, the whole incident again came in front of my eyes. I became scared of even stepping out of the house. Now I clearly understood the meaning of the word hiraeth. It was a beautiful welsh word which means 'a longing for a home you can't return to.' Living that weird school life, living that abhorrent high-class party life of mum and dad's where you have to wear those shiny-fitted dresses in which you can barely breathe, or for that matter living my own life was suffocating me.

When I saw Ayan in school, I planned on telling him everything. He was the closest to what I could call a friend in the school. That feeling to be able to blurt out everything to someone gave my mind an unusual relaxation. However, just when I was going to him, I saw Tia coming to him.

"Ayan I can't believe you are ditching all of us for that aunty. Since when did you start hanging out with such stupid people? Don't you miss us?" Tia punched him on his shoulder.

"Dude, she is nothing more than the perfect vocalist for my band to me. It's just a matter of few days, after this competition I don't know her and she doesn't know me. She isn't as bad as you all think though." Something inside of me just shattered when I heard this. I did not know that I was so insignificant to someone whom I called a friend.

***

After that incident, I never felt safe anywhere apart from my house. It was like I had become phobic to stepping out of the house. I just wanted to live in a small tent in some small corner of my house. Now I just wanted a Lilliput world for me, where there was no space for anyone but me, my thoughts, and my books. Everyone in my family was shocked to see, all of a sudden, such introvert qualities in me. They felt that I was overreacting on the whole shifting thing. But little did they know the bitter truth behind it. I hardly even went for the band rehearsals and managed to make some or the other believable excuse every time.

Practically, after what Ayan said, I shouldn't even be participating anymore. But then what would be the difference betwcen me and him?

***

From the last three days I had been forcefully called to the rehearsals as the competition is tomorrow. Much to my surprise these practices were a great change to me and almost made me forget everything, the only problem being Ayan. Every time I looked at him, it felt he looked back at me with a veil of selfishness.

"What's wrong with you Martins? What about your "keep laughing" policy?" He came to me jumping vibrantly.

"You don't have to pretend to care about me or be nice to me. Despite all your insolence, I am still going to sing for your band." I said dialling dad's number. I didn't care if I was disturbing him but I didn't want to go back with Ayan. Even if that meant going alone.

"Why the heck would I do that? How was your trip by the way? Haven't seen you since." He was a good actor. He could be so cold-hearted inside and pretend as if he really cared about your life or you.

"Dad, can you please come and pick me up from Inayat's place? The practice is over." Avoiding Ayan completely, I asked dad to come and take me home. Just as I was talking to him, I felt my phone being snatched away.

"Good evening uncle, I am Ayan, your daughter's band mate and also your neighbour. Please don't bother, I'll drop her home, I mean I just live next door. See you someday, have a good day. Bye!" This is guy was unbelievable. He sure has led my dad to scold me.

"Aarika, you keep talking about saving the environment, right? Car pooling is one way to do that. So, stop being fussy now and go back home with that gentleman. Mom and I are going to be late today, we have an important meeting. Ask Aafiya to make dinner for you and Kevin. Love you, bye." He didn't even wait for me to say anything and hung up.

"Will you tell me what's wrong with you?" Ayan came and blocked my way.

"No." I pushed him aside and started walking. We didn't speak for the rest of the way and he pretended to change his way in between. But I knew he was walking right behind me and making sure I get home safely. Not because he considered me important in his life, but sure I was important in his band.

***

The much-awaited day was finally here. This competition has changed me much more than I thought. I discovered hidden talents in me and my love for singing. And also, the most important thing, I learnt never to trust anyone or get attached to the wrong people so easily. I wore a red tee paired with black jeggings, as red and black was the dress code of our band. I ditched my big glasses for contact lenses. That thing is surely not meant for clumsy people like me.

"Don't tie your hair today." Mom said, taking away my scrunchie and applying a bit of pink lip gloss on my lips. I haven't let my mom do that to me since I was a kid, but today I am going to let it pass. It's literally every daughter's mother's dream to do this fashion related stuff to their daughters. Even though I hate its smell and taste.

The big auditorium full of people was enough to make me nervous. But then I recalled all the hard-work and efforts we had put to make this performance a success. I looked at my parents with their joyful eyes, I had never seen them this excited. Not for anyone else, I am going to sing for them.

"Wow Martins, you look like a human today, must be an achievement for you." Ayan came to me and said with a wide smile. How unaware he is that I knew what a cold- hearted douche he is.

"Why does everyone look nervous and upset as if someone is dying here? Relax it's just a competition. Winning isn't important, giving our best is. Cheer up now. All the best everyone!" Ayan said with such a wide and vibrant smile. I surely have taught him a lot, changed him drastically from head to toe. From a person who didn't know how to smile to a completely optimistic person. Still he doesn't value my presence in his life. Poor thing. Okay, it's time to stop being a narcissist now.

***

We did not win the competition, we were first runners up. But the satisfaction in everyone's heart was equivalent to winning. Taking into consideration the short span of our practice, we surely did a spectacular job. The song was so beautiful that I had Goosebumps on my arms all the time while singing. I could see how touched everyone was by our performance. Also, I was happy that this is the last day that I ever had to speak to Ayan.

"You did exceptionally well Martins! We all are gathering at Inayat's place, we'll go somewhere to celebrate from there. Be ready at 7, I'll pick you up." I couldn't figure out why Ayan was even inviting me. Now that everything was over, what did he need me for?

"You just needed me for this competition, we don't have any relation beyond that, do we? Friends celebrate. We are not even friends. Weren't we supposed to be done here?" Not even waiting for him to reply I rushed to mom and dad who were eagerly waiting for me with their gleaming eyes. "We are so proud of you sweetie, that was what you call terrific!" Mom hugged me so tightly that she nearly suffocated me to death. But my happiness knows no bounds today so I hugged her even more tightly. "Never knew my daughter was this talented, what else have I missed in all these years?" Dad lifted me in the air just like he used to when

I was two. I was surprised that he still manages to do that. Well one of the perks of being extremely thin.

"Be ready by 7 Martins!" I heard Ayan yelling from the back. That douche actually thinks I am going to go anywhere with him.

***

I did not go to the party that day. Ayan was there at my house sharp at 7 but I made mom tell him that I was down with fever from all the stress and exertion. A blatant lie. After that day all the band members kind of drifted apart and Ayan was back in Tia's group. He did try once or twice to talk to me but I stayed aloof. And I was the loner Aarika again. I didn't regret it much, being alone was better than being in the company of a fake friend.

***

Life wants something else from me. It just can't see me relaxed and content like other normal human beings. When I got back home from the school, I found out that Kevin had met with an accident. The servants at home made me all panicky. They made me feel as if something really serious has happened and he was on his death bed. And I, like a lunatic, broke into tears and started feeling sorry for all the wrongs I had done to him, and how I had spent most of the time away from him even when he wanted my time. I just prayed to God to give him years from my life but not let anything happen to him. But when I reached the hospital, I was so mad and happy at the same time, seeing Kevin laughing as usual. God, what not I had thought and shed so many tears unnecessarily

"Oh, there goes our hero! Sir, I should have brought a cape for you. You are Superman! Or else how could you even think of performing those weird stunts on your stupid bike!" I said sarcastically, scolding Kevin as he cried in pain holding his right arm.

"Aha, there goes my sister trying to copy my cool comments. Well tried, but still you need some practice." He tried to laugh, but was unable to do so due to the wound on his lips.

"Idiot, look what you've done to yourself." I sat for a while with him and then returned home. I was relieved to hear that Kevin had just got nothing else, but some minor fractures and that he would be discharged in ten days.

***

Rather than lollygagging, I was rushing towards the house excitedly. Though it had been the same stressful day at the school, I was excited to meet Kevin after ten long days. As I rang the doorbell the door automatically opened and I was wondering why no one even cared to receive me, and just then I heard a voice come from behind the door and I fell down getting stuck in a long cloth. "Bienvenue a la maison! Didn't get it? Don't worry even I didn't." The voice seemed quite familiar to me, but I still couldn't make out whose voice it was. Then suddenly someone came from behind the door dressed in a whole black outfit with a very unusual long coat like those of superheroes and a very spooky mask of a ghost yelling, "Beware when Don is here!"

I was lost in my thoughts and it's natural that if such a person will see such a scary figure they'll be totally freaked out. "Who are you?" I yelled thumping him with my bag. He looked so spooky that it sent shivers down my spine. Even the Margaret of 'That One Night' didn't scare me to the extent he did. "Kevin! Kevin! Come quickly! There's an intruder in the house!" Hearing my scream Kevin came on his wheel chair and asked me, "What's wrong with you Aarika!? What made your blood run cold?" I could sense something suspicious in his tone as if everything was planned.

"Are you seriously asking this!? Don't you see this abhorrent guy standing in front of you?" Kevin and the boy couldn't control their laughter anymore. "You are such a violent girl Aarika. Shame on you. You shouldn't have behaved like this. We'll have lunch but we'll not order anything for you. Your biggest punishment it will be." Kevin loves making fun of me. It is his most favourite hobby. Seeing me getting infuriated, the boy removed his mask. I was outraged! Those pair of chuck hazel gleaming eyes, that charming smile with a touch of betrayal in it, I had seen it all before. There was an unusual and strange silence for two minutes before I broke out into immense anger. It was Ayan. Who gave that disgusting person the authority to enter my house!

"You? How dare you come here to destroy the peace of my lovely abode! Oh God, you are so childish. Grow up dude. Are you seriously trying to scare me with a stupid mask? Go get a life, bud."

"Look, we've fought as much as we could. It doesn't suit the personality of a peace lover like me. And also, the stranger fact being, I don't even know what you are mad at me for. So, friends?" He brought a hopeful hand towards me.

"What are you doing here?" Addled by his presence at my place, I wondered why all of a sudden, he had shown up. He was the sweet honey, always surrounded by some bee or the other, why would such a guy be at the house of a girl like me. We were just band mates. Oh, I wished he went away instantly.

"Oh, I saw your stupid brother struggling with his wheelchair so I came in to give him a hand. And then he started saying things that I was laughing like lunatics. I had never ever met someone as funny as him."

"Yeah but still less strange than you. Kevin you can text me when your friend's gone. We'll have lunch together." I told Kevin, heading towards the stairs.

"Martins, wait!" I heard him yelling from downstairs.

***

"'*My hands cuffed, my feet tied, here I am in the house of gloom*

This evil of despair has trapped me in its dark room.' Wow, you are quite a writer Martins." As I came out of the bathroom, I saw Ayan sitting on my bed with my diary lying beside him. He was lying so comfortably on my bed as if it was his own.

"How dare you Ayan? You don't know what you have done!" All infuriated, I moved towards him to slap him, but before I could do it, he held my hand and stopped me.

"What's wrong Aarika? Why have you been acting like a lunatic?" I was not used to hearing my first name from him. He must have been really serious at that moment.

"Look I heard what you told Tia about me that day. I thought we were friends, I thought we had a relation beyond just being band mates. I thought I could share my thoughts with you. But you proved me wrong. I am sorry I expected more from you than I should have ever expected." I was not even angry anymore, just hurt.

"I did not know it myself then, Martins. I used to see you just as a freaky girl whom I would never want to talk to. But slowly and steadily this freaky girl changed the meaning of my life, she changed me. And then I realized this freaky girl was exactly the friend I needed. You know, I hadn't cried ever before any of my friends. It was just a common round of jokes with them and nothing else. But you, you are something else. You understood me like no one else. I didn't realize all this until you stopped speaking to me. Your weird jokes added colour to my day, your lunacy, your philosophy made me understand the meaning and purpose of my existence. I miss all of that. I miss you. I am sor.. sorry." That sorry came out a bit hesitantly but I was happy to hear a person like him apologize.

"Well, I do not know what to say. I just know how easy it is for you to have someone or chuck someone out of your life according to your own convenience." I had forgiven him but he was not getting my friendship easily after all the tears I had shed for him.

He took a tissue from the box and makes a ring out of it around my finger. “Aarika Martins, I, Ayan, bent on my knee, propose to you to make me a part of your lunacies. Will you teach me all that freaky, crazy yet cool stuff and make me a complete lunatic?”

“Yes.” My heart did melt there. I was convulsed with laughter after what he did.

“God, I knew you would forgive me if I apologise to you in your way. Well, that’s enough melodrama for one day. Spill the beans now, tell me now what exactly happened. Why did you write all those things in your diary?” For the first time in a very long while, I felt that there’s someone who actually wanted to talk to me.

“Nothing.” I was a bit sceptical if I should tell him or not. After all they were his friends. “You can talk to me, you know? I am not a dinosaur. I won’t swallow you in if you speak.” It just made me feel so good. Without wasting a second, I told him each and everything. Turning on the fan, he removed his shoes and then sat again on my bed comfortably.

“I can’t believe I once called such inhuman people my friends. But don’t you worry, Martins. Wait till tomorrow and then Alisha and her group are out of the school. But promise me, that after tomorrow you won’t say a single thing about the episode. You’ll forget every memory of the past and make new, good memories.” I was shocked that he was ready to take this stand against his friends. There was intensity in his voice. He had begun smiling more often now. For that matter the smile on his face never faded away. It was all so different for having someone talk to me like that when all that others did is mock me.

“You aren’t as bad as I thought, you know,” I said with a smirk on my face, trying to wipe my tears.

“I know. By the way you wrote in your diary that you don’t see any beauty in Mumbai, be ready at ten tonight and I’ll show you what beautiful is.”

"Not tonight please. I don't want to go out." I freaked out a little at the thought of going out. Never ever in worst nightmares had I thought that going out would ever be something that I'll be scared of.

"Look Aarika, you can always get rid of other emotions with determination. But fear, you can never get rid of fear. At every step of your life it wears a different mask and haunts. Sometimes fear wears the mask of insecurity, other times the mask of losing, the mask of being left out. The list is endless. The only way to get rid of it is to fight it in its every form. And that ends my speech, can't be any more philosophical. Alisha or anyone can't trouble you anymore. I am with you now. Trust me, I'll have your back, always. You are not this coward you pretend to be, you are braver than anyone I know. No one has the courage to face whatever you are facing right now."

Hours and hours passed and we didn't even realise it. We were so engrossed in laughing and talking. All that was so new, so good. The feeling was ineffable. After all I realised that life wasn't so bad.

Mom and dad came back from work and they also invited Ayan's mother, Shanaya aunty to dinner.

"Your son is really unprecedentedly nice, Shanaya. He hardly knows Kevin, still he took such great care of him and he also gave Aarika such a great company." Mom told Shanaya aunty what all Ayan did. He really is marvellous. Just next to perfect. "Oh, no need to say thanks dear. He loves to make new friends and I think he's getting along really well with your kids," Shanaya aunty said. She is equally sweet as her son. A very simple and sober lady she is. After having dinner Ayan and I went to my room. It had been six hours, still Ayan had so much stuff to tell and was going on making me laugh.

"What are you going to write in the assignment we got today?" I asked him going through the worksheets. We got an assignment on 'What are your dreams and what they mean to you?' *My Dreams, first, to go to Mussoorie. Second, to never ever come back. Third, maybe take Ayan along. Fourth, to make these dreams come true.*

"I find dreams childish and unrealistic. They are wastage of the present time. Sacrificing the present time in thinking about the future and that too when we aren't even sure if we'll be able to survive the uncertainties of life is utter foolishness. I believe in living in present and making every moment count." He spoke as if he was a mathematician who had already calculated how each second of his life was going to be spent, without a single moment getting wasted.

"You aren't actually going to write that. Are you? God, you are kidding."

"Of course, I am. This is the most important principle of my life. Never to dream, because dreams give rise to expectations, and expectations give rise sadness to most of the times. Just live in the present without the worries of future. And live happily ever after. Time is disloyal to everyone. It will one day take away all our dreams with itself when we die. Why to be the possessor of something which can be taken away?"

"I strongly disagree to that. Isn't life all about dreaming despite all the uncertainties?"

"Wow Miss Philosopher! Come on now, time to go to the place I told you about." He suddenly realised that it was ten, and kept the book back and wore his shoes.

We went to his place where everything was so perfect unlike mine. His room was so well decorated and the walls were black with planets shining in the dark. A hundred photos were hung on the Christmas lights, mostly of beautiful places. He took his violin and woke up his driver. We were soon in front of a huge building. As soon as I got down from the car, my legs started trembling. After a long time I was not among the four walls of my room and I was not liking it. I was scared, doubting Ayan. I wanted to run back. Seeing the colour of my face fade away,

Ayan held my hand. "I won't leave it ever, I promise." Ayan said pointing towards our entwined hands. I felt as if I am a small child again and he is my dad. I never knew before that such a tall building existed in Mumbai. That was the maximum number of stairs I'd climbed. Wheezing and all exhausted we reached the terrace. Ayan put his hands around my eyes even before I got time to breathe. The weather was pleasant and the wind was fierce.

"I am trusting you, promise me, you won't open your eyes before I ask you to." He removed his hands from my eyes and put them on my arms, lifting them up. He opened my hair and whispered in my ear, "You are a bird flying high in the sky, free of all the worries and your hair are your wings, going higher and higher with the wind. Your heart is now the abode of peace and the wind is filling it more and more with its love. Now open your eyes gently." This was so dramatic. Like in movies, it was okay, it adds beauty to the moments. But in real life, oh God! Give me a break. But the surprising fact was, I actually felt like I was flying freely than ever before. I felt as if I'd got wings. The beauty of the moment was ineffable. As I opened my eyes I couldn't decide if I was below the stars or above them. The stars below me were shining equally brightly as those compared to the ones in the sky. The wind was blowing so fiercely, playing with my hair and then kissing my face. I never knew that there was power not just in Ayan's music but in his words too. He started playing the violin and singing along. The feeling that I got is the one which I had almost forgotten in these past days.

"Will you teach me too?" I said pointing towards his violin.

"Well that'll depend on your dedication, child." He said in a mature voice and laughed.

***

The next day Ayan accompanied me to the principal's office. I narrated each and every thing that those bunch of morons did to me and I tried hard to control my tears, but that only made the situation seem more serious to Principal Donna. I told her how bad I had been all that while and she insisted on sending me to the school counsellor. But I didn't think that anyone could counsel me better than Ayan, so I refused. I never knew that Principal Donna was this sensitive towards matters like these. Her furrowed eyebrows hinted anger. "I will not let them go so easily!" She roared with uncontrollable fury. She made a call to Alisha's parents and talked to them so calmly as if she was calling them to her office not to punish their child, but award her. The same way the whole group's parents were informed.

Soon the parents gathered around the principal's desk. Heads held high, constantly looking at their watches, they looked at each other, as if completely unaware of their children's deeds or for that matter as if they had almost forgotten that their children even exist. "Well none of you look concerned enough to know why you've been called here. So, I won't take much of your time, you can pick your dear children and no need to send them here ever again." Principal Donna's bloodshot eyes scared the wits out of everyone. Her words were a sudden alarm to all the parents who had been sleeping until now. But the regret, the fear, the worry was seen on none of their faces.

This brought a sudden realisation to me. If those kids were left in the hands of such people, their lives would be ruined. At least with Principal Donna they had a scope of improvement. I couldn't let that happen just because of me. "No ma'am, please, that will be too much. I would like to give them another chance. Just a few hours in the locked store room of our school would be enough. I see it hasn't been cleaned for a while now. They should know what it feels like to be there so that they don't have the audacity to send anyone else there ever. That would be enough for me." I didn't know why I was doing it for them, but this seemed the best to me at that time.

"If you request so dear, I'll set them free. But remember if they repeat it, I have your back, always. And you all learn something from her. And oh, my dear parents or should I say party animals,

I would really appreciate if from now on your children are your concern and not those meaningless parties. You may leave now." A bit calmed down, she pointed towards the door.

"And Aarika, I am proud of you." She smiled at me.

Just in a few hours I felt that my life had been set straight. Ayan seemed like an angel in person to me right now. The path that I had left behind was grassy with thorns hidden in it, but I hoped that the path in front of me would be all flowery. And with Ayan by my side I was even ready to face the thorns.

"Happy now, Martins? And your music classes start from today, sharp at 4, my place." Ayan pulled my hair and beamed a smile at me.

"You idiot, you'll make me bald someday," I said, tying my hair again.

"Oh my God, it's so funny to imagine you bald. Your head looks so big. If you ever become bald, I really wish I am the reason for it. Oh, my stomach hurts." He was laughing so hard holding his stomach that he was barely able to even breathe. We went back to the class and it wasn't the same hell that it was yesterday. Everything around me seemed so beautiful.

His coming to my life wasn't like the entrance of any person, but the entrance of liveliness and happiness. And I hoped that happiness stayed forever.

2008
What just happened?

Late in the seventeenth year of my life I realized how frabjous my life had turned. Ayan fulfilled his promise; he did make me fall in love with my life in no more than three years. I didn't even realise how these three years passed while singing, dancing and doing all the crazy things. At last I learned how to laugh and enjoy even the smallest things happening around. It was as if a miracle had happened to a blind and he could see the world of joy once again. I cannot say that my teen life was perfect but yes, I can say that with Ayan I got the courage to walk on the bed of difficulties. No matter how much you try, you can never escape problems. They are inevitable. All it takes is one crazy person to help you enjoy even the most difficult moments of your life.

In these three years I also made quite a lot of progress in playing the violin. Though Ayan never agrees with that. Things which are perfect according to me demand to be a lot better according to him. He is surprisingly quite strict as a teacher.

We have had a very tiring day at school today.

Both of us had taken our last exam of eleventh class and now it was finally time for a long and relaxing break, probably the only thing we've looked forward to in the past two months. We watched 'That One Night' for the thousandth time but it seemed equally scary to me as it was when I watched it for the first time. The ghost doesn't actually exist but the protagonist just hallucinates. She doesn't realise when her fear turned into something as scary as hallucinations. That's the thing about fear. Each passing day with us it grows, how to kill it nobody knows.

"Are you still scared of this movie?" Ayan drew all my attention towards him and that is when a disembodied voice came from the T.V., the screen went blank and within a gap of two seconds, creepy Margaret with blood stains on her pale whitish grey skin yelled in her spookiest voice. But what I did as a result was even creepier. I threw the cup of coffee right on the T.V. screen and gave a deafening scream. Kevin came with a long stick in his hand, all set to smack me. "Wow that's what I wanted!" Ayan exclaimed as he saw me in a state of fear. "Kevin, are you seriously going to hit your cute little sister?" I said in a soft voice and made a face as innocent as a lamb, while making efforts to control my laughter.

"Sorry madam, but you are in a total misconception," Kevin replied with an evil smile on his face.

"Why?"

"This stick is for a psycho who had run away from the mental hospital a few years ago and she is now giving her best to make more and more people just like her" Anything is possible in this wicked world but Kevin will never stop passing such ludicrous comments. But I was really going to miss him as I would see his tomfoolery for just a few days more and then he'll be gone to London for higher studies. It's queer that in addition to being impish, how brainy he is. He got a scholarship for an aerospace engineering course in The University of Glasgow.

"Kevin, I totally agree with you," Ayan and Kevin again started mocking me and I sat in one corner of the house with a poker face. Kevin walked away and Ayan came to me. "Sorry for what all I did. But I promise you won't be gnashing your teeth after where I'll take you tonight."

"Sorry sir, but I am not going anywhere with you."

"Okay then I'll go with Alisha and Tia."

"Huh. Idiot. But where are we going?"

"That's a surprise but be ready by 12 a.m."

"12 a.m.! Are you kidding?"

"The true pleasure of that place is in the night only."

"Do I have any option, rather than going? Anyway, I'll be there."

"Okay, see you then!"

"Bye!"

Everyone knows how gullible I am, of which they always take advantage. I was filled with a variety of emotions. Confused, exasperated, frightened and excited, all at the same time.

“Aarika dear, is anything troubling you?” Dad asked. I ate dinner at the table just like a guilty person does after committing a crime. Though I hadn’t done anything yet, but the guilt of sneaking out at twelve is killing me. It was already ten and I could barely breathe. After so much effort I finally found the burkha that I had purchased for the school play. That was the best I could do to prevent anyone from seeing me.

***

It was 11:58 p.m. when my phone rang. “Hey Aarika, open the window and come down quickly!” It was Ayan. On one hand was him, who was always so peppy but then also he had never ever sounded so excited, and on the other hand was me, whose condition was worse than a drowning and helpless person.

“You douche bag, you expect me to jump from the third floor, am I a ball that you will catch easily or Spiderman who has supernatural powers?” I replied, all freaked out.

“You nincompoop! First see and then speak. There’s a ladder. You have to come down with its help. Nobody is asking you to become a ball or Spiderman.”

“Oh...okay... I am sorry!” I somehow managed to get down even with that oversized burkha. “Du siehstsehrblod!” he grunts.

“What? Did you just confess that you are a psychiatric hospital runaway?”

“No idiot, it means you look really funny in German.” He smirked.

“Oh, you look no less, my unicorn. Wait, what are you up to?” He rummaged through the things in his bag and took out his phone.

"Nothing, just capturing some rare pics of an alien. Have a look." He handed me his phone with a super funny picture of me in it.

"God, Ayan you are so dead."

We sat in his mom's car and the moment he started driving, it felt as if a plane was taking off. The night had never seemed so frightening and dark. Everyone has some supernatural powers. My supernatural powers are that I can sense beforehand what is going to happen and this time I am totally sure that I am not going to return home, and even if I do, I wouldn't be in my right senses. It has only been ten minutes but still I can't wait for more. I can feel the heat inside me. Even the fully air-conditioned car was just like mercury to me. My body was trembling and I was feeling suffocated at the same time.

"Stop the car!" I whooped on the top of my voice but it doesn't make any difference. The amplitude of the music is such that my voice is just a whale's cry. So, I had no other option than punching him. "What was that for? Do you want to die or want to end up being in the jail? You know what it means to distract a driver?" He scolded me.

"Look Ayan, please take me back. I don't want to die so early." I begged of him to take me back but ignoring what all I said, he simply drove even faster.

***

After several attempts of convincing Ayan, with each of them failing, we finally reached the Rainbow Park, which is said to be the worst park of Mumbai. "At 12 in the night you got no place to bring me except for this weird park? Seriously Ayan, I am so disappointed in you. This wasn't a good joke." I am so mad at him for bringing me here that I don't even realize that I step on my own burkha and fall down. And as I fall down my hand lands on another hand and when I turn the torch towards it, I find that it is a white hand completely drained of blood. "How dare you bring me here!?" I screamed.

"Stop being so impatient and give that hand to me!"

"Okay take it, I already knew that you were a vampire or something, so obviously such things are going to fascinate you. Take it, all yours. You have fun with your beloved ghosties here, I am going back."

"Okay bye," he said breaking that hand.

"Wait, how did you break the hand?"

"Idiot it's not a real hand. It's made of wax. It is drained in red paint not blood. You still don't want to go? Okay I'll enjoy."

"What if there's nothing?"

"What if there's everything?"

"Don't you know that this place is said to be haunted?"

"What if they are just superstitions?"

"I know you'll not agree. So, let's not waste our time here and go inside." I had to agree, for even if I leave, how would I reach my home. I didn't know how to drive. What is the worst that could happen? I could die. Never mind. Worse things have already happened to me.

Though the name of the place is Rainbow Park, it is a jungle and not a park. We switched on our torches and started walking. There was nothing except for tall bushy trees that I could see. "You seriously brought me here to see these trees? The garden outside my house wasn't enough for that?" I complained when we had walked for almost an hour but didn't see anything worth coming here. My feet were paining and I was all sweaty. But when I didn't hear any reply coming I turned around to see why it was so. Ayan was sitting on the ground with both his hands on the stomach. His face clearly stated that he was in a lot of pain. He was wheezing too. Seeing that, I rushed quickly towards him, frantically.

"What's wrong with you? What happened all of a sudden? Are you all right?" I asked while helping him to get up.

"Yes, I am fine. Don't worry. It's just the humid weather that is making me feel so sick," he replied in an extremely low voice.

"Ayan you don't look so good. We'll come here again later. But for now, let's go back, please."

"No after coming such a long way we can't go back just like this, without even seeing anything. I am totally fine."

"Okay, as you plead sir."

Ayan got up with a lot of difficulty but his movement wasn't normal. It was like that of a dancing man. He was laughing so I thought that he was doing this to make me laugh. We walked for another one hour but didn't see anything except some wild animals and a few homeless people sleeping. After seeing some of them, I was confused if that is a short sleep or they had slept forever. But I was too scared to go and check. I just wanted to see that mysterious place that Ayan had been babbling about for so long. As we kept walking further, the curiosity grew more and more.

After walking for almost two hours, we finally saw something different. A cave sort of thing, the only place in the jungle through which a little bit light was coming. As we walked through the cave, I couldn't believe my eyes. I seriously felt that while walking I had fallen asleep and all that was a dream. There were beautiful bioluminescent trees and flowers. All of them are so pretty and colourful. There were glow worms all around. Between them was a narrow lake in which there were numerous beautiful aquatic plants.

Breeze so cool, grass so green

Being there felt no less than a dream.

It was so enchanting that I wanted to scream

My eyes were all teary but with a gleam.

I was all weary but that sight helped me to become fresh

It all even became more blissful when the tiny rain drops touched my flesh.

I threw my bag and all the things in my hand and started dancing to the beat of the drops falling on the ground. The wet grass calmed all my stressed nerves. The stars above twinkled. The sweet chirping of the birds added to the beauty of the moment. It felt as if they were singing us some melodious songs in their own beautiful language. I just wanted to stay there forever. If it was a dream, I never wanted to wake up. Ayan too sat beside me. "Miss Martins, got anything to say now? Or do you still want to exterminate me?"

"Thank you, thank you is all I can say. I don't have any more words. You made me see something that I wouldn't have seen on my own ever."

"Dad brought me here and taught that we never want to go in the depth of anything. No matter what it is like, our eyes will always be deceived by the outer side and it's always the outer side that forces us to give up, but it's on us what we want. Do a little effort and see the truth or convince ourselves to always accept what is shown to us. I miss him so much! I wish he was alive, here with us. Very few people know about this place. The rest just think that those people are kidding." He took a deep breath. To divert his attention, I cracked a few jokes. We laughed for another few minutes and then wallowed in our heavenly environment. I closed my eyes and felt the gentle breeze touch my skin and play with my hair.

"Hey, Aarika listen. I want to tell you something. I..." I could just hear him whisper this much. After that I couldn't even hear anything, and fell asleep.

***

I was woken up soon by a strange sound. As I woke up, I heard Ayan sobbing. I couldn't see his face as he was facing the opposite side. I rubbed my eyes, got up and went to him. "Ayan, did anything happen? What's wrong?" He turned towards me and gave me a tight slap. That wasn't a friendly slap, but a very serious one. He didn't stop before giving me five to six slaps like that. I even got a big scratch on my face from the ring he was wearing. "Stay away from me!" He pushed me, picked up his bag, and started walking back to the cave. I stood there with my hand on my cheek, thunderstruck.

I didn't even realize when such a bright night took such a bad shade. The fact that he slapped me didn't scare me, but the fact that his hands were craving to hurt me more; the fact that I had become afraid of my own best friend scared the shit out of me. But I didn't say anything. Not a single word. I thought that he was missing his dad that's why he behaved in such a way or maybe there are seriously some spirits that got into him. He too didn't say anything on our way back. I reached my room through the same ladder. It was five in the morning. I got into my quilt and burst into tears, but in no less than fifteen minutes I fell asleep. After a few hours there was a knock on my door. "Aarika! Aarika open the door. Sunday doesn't mean that you'll sleep the whole day. Wake up! It's eleven already," mom shouted.

I got up and sat on my bed. Incidents from the previous night started replaying in my brain. A part of me wanted to slap Ayan back and ask him how dare he do so, but a part of me cared for him and wants to know what made him do it. As I opened the door mom started examining me from head to toe. Continuing to examine me she asked, "How did you get that scratch honey? And why are you wearing that Burkha?" This makes the hair on the back of my neck stand up. It is so silly of me to do something like this. That night was such a terrifying ordeal that it made me forget everything.

"Mom I don't know for what reason I wasn't feeling well and really cold and I couldn't find any extra quilt or anything to cover myself, so I didn't have any other option."

"Wow here we are dying of this deadly hot summer and there you want to cover yourself with layers and layers of clothes.

Search for some more practical excuse next time. And what explanation do you have for that scratch?

“And next time whenever you feel cold you can just turn off the fan. That would be more practical,” mom said suspiciously not getting her eyes off me.

“You know mom once I am fast asleep, I have no track of what’s going on around me. Also, I was practicing geometry last night and I didn’t care to remove my things so I must have got hurt from one of those many things.” I replied while feeling the big scratch against my fingertips.

“Come and sit with me for a while,” is all that mom replied. Mom and I went to her room and sit on the bed. Mom placed her hand on my lap and asked in her softest voice, “Is there something that is troubling you honey?”

“No, I am absolutely fine mom.” I said trying to control my tears so hard. How could I tell her that yes, a lot is troubling me, my best friend, my only friend had hurt me so badly and that too after giving me the biggest joy.

“Are you sure you aren’t hiding anything Aarika. Even if it’s bad tell me. I am your mother and I should know each and everything about you, don’t make me feel like a stranger.” She asked in a serious tone.

“Chill mom, it’s just a scratch. If something will happen, I’ll never hide it. Now I should go and have a shower,” I got up and started walking out of the room. I heard mom yelling from behind, “Please take care of yourself, I don’t want to see even a single scratch on you.”

“Thanks mom! I will.”

I felt so loved but guilty at the same time for hiding things. What right do cheaters like us have to lie to our parents, to shatter their trust? What right do we have to shout at the ones, the only ones who don’t mind sacrificing their lives for us? Wanting to puke my emotions I went to Kevin’s room. “Kevin! Kevin are you awake? If yes then please let me in?" I said knocking on his door. I heard his footsteps and breathe a sigh of relief. "Whoa! What a rare sight of a monkey chattering right outside my room! Not seen monkeys in a while. Thanks for visiting. Come in. I'll get you some bananas." Kevin looked really happy to see me because I rarely talk to him or spend time with him. So that is truly a rare sight for him. "Kevin, I want to tell you something but only if you promise to keep it a secret."

"I promise. I'll never let the cat out of the bag." Though Kevin is a big jerk, he is a trustworthy person and most probably the best person at the moment to give me perfect guidance. So, I narrated each and every incident of the night to him from how we reached there, what we saw, and how we came back, including what Ayan did. "I already knew that something was wrong with this guy. The best thing for you to do is right now is not jump to any conclusions. There's a reason behind everything we do. Does it hurt a lot?" he said pointing at my scratch. Maybe this was the first time in these seventeen long years when I saw Kevin serious. It felt good.

"Not more than my heart. I just want you to tell me what should I do? Go talk to him, not speak a word to him or forget everything?" Tears roll down my cheeks as I reminisce what all happened. I don't want to lose such a great friend. "Let's go and talk to him and clarify everything. But I am telling you there are serious problems going on with him. No joke intended this time," Kevin said.

I meet Ayan almost daily but today I had the same feeling that I used to have whenever mom and dad or anyone forced me to talk to a stranger. When Kevin and I went outside to go to Ayan's house we saw Ayan and dad already sitting in the garden. They were laughing so hard. The weather was still lovely. The smell of the rain was mixed with grass, cool breeze was still blowing, but the difference was just that it didn't please me like it did yesterday. "Good morning kids! Come join us. Your friend has such a good sense of humour. He's been making me laugh for so long." Dad called us, trying so hard to control his laughter. Why wouldn't he enjoy Ayan's company? They are so similar to each other. But let's not forget to acknowledge the fact that he never slapped me like Ayan did.

"Hey potato! Long time no see? That scratch looks really funny." Ayan came running towards me with his smiling face as if nothing has happened or as if he has completely forgotten what he did. He even forgot giving me that scratch. Kevin was about to say something but I stopped him. Seeing him behave normally I wanted to forget everything, thinking that he may have hit me as a joke and I created a big fuss about it. "Hey!" I replied.

"Kevin, Aarika, why don't you guys come to my place today? That would be so much fun!" Kevin and I stood there in shock, unable to figure out any connection between his actions. Kevin looked at me waiting for my suggestion about what to do next. I signalled him not to say anything and took the charge of replying. "Sure, we'll be there, but after having dinner. Kevin will be leaving tomorrow and a lot of packing is still left."

"Oh, yeah, I totally forgot about it. Okay, see you!"

Rest of the day we didn't talk about Ayan. Once we started packing, we completely lost track of time and didn't even realize when the ten in the morning turned to ten in the night. We had dinner and as we promised Ayan, it was time to go to his place. "Come Kevin, Ayan will be waiting for us." As I went to his room I saw his teary eyes. He was looking at our old family picture. "Kevin, don't be so upset. Going there will only make your career." I wiped his tears and took the picture from his hand.

"It's easy for you to say but just imagine how it is to be in a country of totally different people, totally different surroundings, totally different culture, and that too without you all! Just imagine what I am going to do there." He was hardly able to speak. Tears continued rolling down his cheeks.

"You are just going to study the subject that you have been crazy about since you were eight and keep eating bananas in the memory of this monkey," as I said that, Kevin's eyes were swimming in mirth.

"Now come on, Ayan is waiting for us."

***

"Hey Ayan open the door we are here." The door was shut and we had been ringing the bell for so long but no one came to open the door. We had been waiting for ten minutes but when no one came, we decided to go back. But then suddenly Shanaya aunty opened the door. She looked really pale. Her watery eyes called out for help. "I don't think you should go inside right now. Ayan isn't well. Please go back," she said in a soft voice and then broke out into tears. "No, aunty we'll not go back until we meet Ayan, and we are definitely not going to leave you in this condition," Kevin said in a stern voice.

We made her sit down and asked what is wrong several times, but she didn't utter a single word. She sat still. I went to the kitchen to bring a glass of water for her. As I was coming back, a heavy vase fell from above, right beside me. Had I been five or ten centimetres to the right I wouldn't have been alive or would have got serious head injuries. I stood still and looked upwards. I was rooted to the spot when I saw Ayan bringing another heavy piece of furniture to throw on my head. He was crying and yelling as if he was possessed by some demonic spirits. "Ayan! What are you doing?" I screamed putting both my hands on my head and running away. "Kids hurry up and leave. Just go without asking any questions. Please go!" Shanaya aunty pushed us towards the gate and started crying even louder.

"We can't leave you like this aunty, what if this lunatic hurts you too?" Kevin yelled, all apoplectic.

"You piece of shit leave my house right now! And you a dumb, boring, seventy-kilogram hideous girl, never show me your face again!" Ayan said breaking another show piece.

Let's keep everything aside, I have been called so many things but seventy kilograms!? I never was and never will be. We couldn't figure out what to do. To leave Shanaya aunty alone would be a foolish thing to do, but to stay there and risk our lives seemed even more foolish. It was ironic how I was running away from the guy who once saved my life. "Kevin, listen we can't go back like this. Be absolutely normal. Mom is already very tensed about us."

"I swear if he comes in front of me again he'll not go back alive. But also, I am really worried about Shanaya aunty. What has gotten into him! He was absolutely fine yesterday." For the first time I saw Kevin actually angry. On the other hand, he looked like he'll break into tears any moment.

"I am not at all mad at Ayan, but I am really worried about him. I have known him for two years, spent my complete days with him. I know he cannot do this."

"But he already did that, Aarika."

"It wasn't him. Something made him do that. Something that was very serious. Something we need to go in depth of. He is that sweet guy who can't see a single drop of tear even in his enemy's eyes. Why would he do that?"

"No, we don't need to go in depth of anything. And sometimes there are no answers to certain things. If there were, so many 'whys' wouldn't have been left unanswered. And I will go tomorrow, after that, promise me that you'll never meet that deranged lunatic ever again."

"NO! Please I cannot do that! Don't you know that if I have any friend in this whole world then it is Ayan! And when you'll be gone, whom will I talk to? The walls?" I moved back from Kevin and started yelping at him. I was shocked to see such a reaction as he has always been a very wise person, but today I wonder where his wisdom had gone.

"Is your entertainment more precious or your life?" he asked rudely.

"There's no life without entertainment, so of course entertainment is more precious."

"Aarika, this isn't a movie going on here. This is reality, and the reality is that Ayan can hurt you, and if you meet him again, he will definitely hurt you. He is not in his right senses. Come out of your world of fantasy and grow up!" He held my arms tightly and started screaming at me.

"But that doesn't mean I'll never meet him again. Leaving him is like leaving all my happiness, and I have realized how important happiness is in one's life."

"Aarika, I never wanted to take this step but now you've compelled me. I'll tell all my friends here to keep an eye on you, and if they ever see you going to his place or him coming to ours, they'll tell each and everything to mom." He blackmailed me so easily and went inside the home as if nothing had happened. I fell down on my knees and started crying in the middle of the road like a hungry beggar. I was hungry. For my friendship.

I felt so weak, weak to fight back, weak to get up and go back to my house. Tears blurring my eyes, I didn't even realise that a truck was speeding towards me, neither did I see that drunk man driving his car towards me with an uncontrollable speed. But the truck driver was just in time to stop his truck and save my life. I heard many passers-by swearing at me until I finally got up and went back.

***

"Kevin dear, take care of yourself and make the best use of the opportunity you've got. We are really proud of you son." Mom told Kevin, hugging him. "And no bike riding in London. If you really want to show off something, show off your marks not your stunts." Dad laughed. "And make use of this technology to communicate with us also not just your friends." Mom joined dad in laughter. But I don't utter a single word, or for that matter don't even look at him. I am mad at him for leaving me alone and also, I am mad at him for not letting me talk to Ayan. Shanaya aunty was standing in the balcony, drinking coffee and looking a bit relaxed. I really wished that I could ask her about Ayan but couldn't. Mom, dad and I said hello to her, and Kevin showed her a thumbs up and she nodded back.

"Won't you say anything Aarika? And don't worry about Ayan. I went to Shanaya aunty's place. Everything is fine." Kevin looked at me surprisingly as I had not spoken a word. I still didn't say anything and walked inside the house, intentionally ignoring what he said. "What's wrong with this girl?" Mom said. "Sometimes even I fail to understand that," dad replied. I watched them from the window as I didn't want to face anyone. "Oh, nothing dad, she's just a bit mad at me. Anyway, it's time to go now, taxi has been waiting for long and tell that idiot I said goodbye." Kevin left. All my joy too left with him. I felt as hollow in my heart as I used to feel three years ago. Sometimes some people come into our lives who give us the biggest joys, but when they leave it feels just like they have stabbed us and gone.

2008
Changing
colours

"It's very beautiful there, I don't know where 'there' is but I believe it's somewhere and I hope it's beautiful."

It's been three months since Kevin has gone. As I expected, my life has turned exactly the same as it was two years ago, boring and dull. It's not that I didn't try to meet Ayan. I tried but Shanaya aunty won't just let me in or make the silliest of excuses. Despite knowing what it could lead me to, I tried. A thousand times I tried. In life we take some risks not because we are not afraid, but because we have, not much, but just a little more love than fear for it. And in the end, every time, love is what mattered because each time it overpowered fear.

But it seems that love winning this battle with fear, me gathering my nerves, is futile. Hours have turned into days, days into weeks and weeks into months, but I haven't met Ayan. Kevin appointed people to keep an eye on me but he had forgotten that Ayan and I studied in the same school. But lucky Kevin, I didn't see him there either. Each moment I would wait, hope that maybe someday, sometime I would see my best friend again until something happened.

"Ayan! Wait! Don't run Ayan!" I finally saw him after like a hundred years. But he ignored me and started walking towards Alisha. "Alisha, would you do me a favour and tell this girl to stop following me. It freaks me out." I couldn't believe my ears. "This girl." "This girl" was once everything to him, and now he was talking about me as if I was some spooky stranger. For the first time in my life I saw Alisha smiling at me. And this time I am quite sure that it was not a mocking smile. I know how miraculous Ayan's company is. It can transform a person from head to toe.

***

My bad days weren't so bad just because of one person. Mayra, the new girl in school. I didn't pity her for being bullied. I pitied the people who bullied her for they lost the opportunity to know someone as cool and fun as Mayra. She too was quite alone in the school like me. Maybe that's why she felt my pain. Maybe she was the new beginning to my life.

It was my final year in school. I could either pursue my dreams or lament over Ayan and Kevin. Ayan was just there in my life for three years. But my parents were there for me all the time. I just couldn't shatter their dreams like this. In the time which I used to spend with Ayan, I started hanging out with Mayra and joined music classes. Mayra is a great girl. She actually helped me to forget about Ayan and Kevin. Or maybe it was because I didn't hear Ayan's voice anymore or saw him in school anymore.

***

"Come Aarika, they are good for nothing. Don't waste your time on them." Mayra took me away while I was having a fight with Kabir, who was teasing me for being a loner again. It's been four months and Mayra has helped me to reform myself.

"Did you give your name for the music fest?" Mayra asked.

"Nope I didn't. I am in no mood to perform for such shitty people. Did you?"

"Yeah, I did. You don't have to sing for them but for yourself. Hey how about you singing your song 'Hold my hand forever' and I give it the background music?" She said in an elevated voice and held my hand.

"No, I cannot sing for so many people! I just can't! I know I'll go blank on the stage." I made an excuse as I just did not want to participate with so much happening in life, Mayra of course didn't know that I was a part of the band a year back. So, making silly excuses, I begged of her to not force me.

"I didn't know that you had the ability to predict things. Why do you go for so many classes then? To sing to the walls?" Everyone knows that a little bit of persuasion and Aarika will say yes. This time too I said yes, but I just didn't have a heart for it.

***

A week had passed by and only three days are left for the fest. Mayra prepared me well and gave amazing music to my song. Though I had sung many a time with my band, but never my own school. And singers here made me much more nervous, as everyone already hated and made fun of me. One single mistake and these people would make my life hell for the rest of the year.

***

The day had finally arrived. My dress was ready, my song was ready and finally, I was ready. I realized that if I didn't go I wouldn't do justice to myself and my talent. I was wearing a black shimmery floor length gown with my hair tied in a messy bun. The biggest mistake of the day was that I wore mom's pencil heels. I hadn't worn any kind of heels before. I desperately needed some motivation and approval of the one who made my singing so much better. I couldn't get it from anyone else but Ayan. So, I left all my ego, Kevin's promise, and mom's fear behind, and decided to go to his place. I had reached my saturation point and couldn't torture myself anymore. But with as much excitement that I marched to his home, I came back with much more disappointment. As I went there, I found the house locked. When the watchman saw me standing there, he came to me.

"Madam they don't live here now. They have left."

"For how long?"

"I don't think they'll come back ever again. Shanaya madam told me to call her if I ever saw someone trying to harm the house or any uncanny activity going in or around the house. But the number she gave is not of India."

"When did they leave?"

"Almost two months ago." Two months! They left so silently that no one ever got to know. They didn't even care to tell anyone. Four years of friendship, and Ayan didn't even stop by to say goodbye one last time. He left so many mysteries for me to solve. Those mysteries to which nobody had an answer, except him. Though I haven't talked to Ayan for almost a year, but still I had a satisfaction that he was living just next to me. A ray of hope that I'll someday, sometime get to see him. But that hope too was gone now. It was as if I was a mirror and he threw a stone on me and went. I was a fractured mirror. No matter how many marvellous facets and rainbows would be produced but ultimately, I would remain something that was broken.

"Mom, did you know that Ayan and Shanaya aunty moved out?" I went back to the house with anger in my eyes. How could I not know this?

"Of course, I do. Everyone does, not that anyone cares." Mom said so casually, as if it's the last thing that she's bothered about.

"How could you not tell me, mom! How could you be so casual about it? Isn't Shanaya aunty your friend?" I yelled at her for maybe the first time in my life.

"Stop screaming Aarika! It's not my fault that you keep yourself locked in those four dark, depressed walls of your room, with absolutely no idea of your surroundings." She was right, I never got out of my room. But still, her answer didn't satisfy me.

"This is no reason for you not telling me, mom! We talk about so many useless things, why couldn't you talk to me about this? Didn't you know what Ayan was to me?" My tears had turned into anger now.

"What do you think Aarika, that I didn't know what was going on between you and Kevin? I overheard you. I didn't want that crazy fellow to be around you! If this is what I get for caring about you, then I am sorry!" She shouted back, even louder.

"Bullshit!" I screamed throwing the vase kept on the table.

I didn't have much time so I rushed to the school. When I reached the auditorium, Kyra was performing. And after two people it was my performance. Mayra saw me and happily waved at me, but that day for the first time while looking at her I felt that she'll leave me too. Just like Ayan, Kevin, Alisha, and all others who left me. I again sank into the pool of my thoughts in which all the memories of the past three years were swimming. But it seemed as if they didn't know how to swim, so they couldn't last for long and soon drowned.

However, all this helped me in a way today. All the fear of performing on the stage was gone. Only pain and anger was left. They announced my name on the stage. Mayra started playing the guitar and I was just about to sing, but thanks to my pencil heels, I had a great fall. There was a deafening silence for two minutes before everyone broke into laughter. But my eyes didn't see anyone. My ears didn't hear anyone. My body didn't feel any sensation but just the thoughts of what happened float in my head.

I simply got up and ignored everyone and started to sing. My mood was just perfect for the song. It is my first self-written song. As soon as I finished singing, the lights were switched on and I could see tears in almost everyone's eyes including mine. Some started shouting 'once more' while some started singing the chorus. I was stunned to see such a response to my performance. I had never seen such admiration or respect for me in anyone's eyes. But still this didn't help me to forget what I saw that day. "It's time to announce today's winners. Any guesses who the first prize is bagged by?" The announcement was made after shreya's performance.

"Aarika! Mayra! Aarika! Mayra!" everyone cheered.

"Yes, absolutely right! The first prize goes to Aarika and Mayra!"

"Thank you everyone!" Mayra and I said in unison, accepting the trophy.

"Man! You were awesome! You know what was better than your song? The way you handled the situation and the feelings you sang with today." Mayra came running after me as I was heading for the house.

"You know what Mayra? You can also leave me alone. No need to run after me anymore. You are going to get bored of me and leave me one day or the same can happen to me as well. So, it's better to make that day today and leave each other alone before we get more attached to each other. And here, you can have this trophy." I was so hurt that I replied like the meanest girl alive. Before she could say anything, I quickly ran towards my house. I had lost my trust and interest in humanity. *Is this what you get for being a good friend? Do feelings like love and care actually exist?* Even if they did, I had stopped believing in them.

He said that he'll hold my hand forever

He said that he'll let me go never

He shall not think that abandoning me was clever

Because someday he'll go through the same tremor.

I can forget him but not the memories we had

Not because I want to cherish them but I don't want to repeat them so that I can be glad.

Part of me wants him to get a slap

But he shall not worry because life will fulfil my wish and then I will clap.

But if I hope so I will be the same

And what will come to me is shame.

So, I just have one thing to pray

That for what all he did he never has to pay

Because I am his friend and I'll never betray.

For the next few days, forgetting everything I devoted myself completely to studies. Things got better with Mayra too. I apologized to her for trying to punish her for someone else's mistakes. Had it not been for her I wouldn't even have gotten the courage to study with so much going on in my mind. I don't know where all I went, I have lost the count of people from whom I inquired about Ayan. But the shocking fact was that no one knew what had happened to him, where he had gone.

All the exams went really well and a month later the results were declared. I was amazed to see that my state rank was second. I was extremely happy to see the pride in mom and dad's eyes, but also after the fest I had made some decisions for myself. I was adamant not to change them. "I am so proud of you my darling daughter! Now you can easily study law in a good college!" Mom was so excited; I had never seen such happiness on her face. But soon that happiness was going to turn into anger.

"Sorry mom you are mistaken. Not law, I can study music in a good college."

"What are you saying Aarika, have you lost your mind?" Dad said very casually as if he was seriously thinking that I was joking.

"No dad, I am absolutely all right. What will happen to me?"

"Then how can you even think of ruining your career?" Mom said in a raised voice.

"Mom, I came second, which means I am not the best at it, but I promise to come first in the field of music. You've never heard me sing or play guitar, that is why you are thinking that what I am talking is nonsense. Believe me mom, you'll be much prouder of me than you are today."

"Aarika you were so clear about your career for so many years. Who stuffed your mind with this shit?" Mom was extremely angry. She started scolding me and tried her best to convince me to change my mind. But luckily my parents are not one of those who forcibly make their children do something in which they have no interest. So, after six hours of debating, squabbling, persuading, fighting, mom and dad finally relented. I applied to various universities and finally my application to Oxford University got shortlisted. Maybe this was the time for new beginnings. Maybe there can't be anything better than going to a college in London. Maybe I'll finally get to live a peaceful life. Maybe.

2009
Fun time!
London time!

Finally, after so many persecutions I was in London. London is a perfect city. The kind of city I have always dreamt of. The trains, the people, the smell of the snow, the roads, the clouds, everything is so beautiful! I have been to various countries, but there is something different about London. Coming here brought me a painful realization. As much as I hate accepting it, but I have grown up. Now I have to complete this journey alone. Mom, Dad, Kevin, no one is going to hold my hand anymore as I walk through this biting cold wind.

Kevin, I have to meet Kevin today. I had completely forgotten about my fight with him but as soon as I think of him that fight too crops up into my mind. All of a sudden, I started feeling awkward as it had been two years since I last spoke to him. Each time he came back to the house, I never uttered a word. He tried calling me a thousand times but I didn't pick up even one of his calls. For some reason I always blamed him for what happened. Had he not stopped me, I wouldn't have to wake up each morning in mystery and suspense and try to solve the intricate maze of Ayan's life. But maybe, some relations, some friendships are not meant to be. Though Ayan was more than just my best friend, my family, I had to forget him. Maybe even if Kevin wouldn't have stopped me, I wouldn't have gotten the answers to my questions. So, I decided to move on in life and forgive Kevin as well. I planned to give him a surprise.

***

"Kevin, are you there?" I rang the doorbell and knocked the door. An unknown face opened the door. "Hi!" I went to Kevin while he was really engrossed in his studies.

"You! Why have you come here!?" He was really shocked to see me and became unexpectedly angry. Well, he had all the reasons to be mad at me because this time it was me who was at fault and not Kevin. "Uh okay I'll leave." I felt really awkward and decided that it would be better to let mom and dad handle the situation, and I should stay in a hotel for some days.

"Idiot, stop!" Kevin came and hugged me tightly.

"Thanks for letting me stay." I hugged him back too.

"You, dork brain! Had you become the prime minister of India? Or started doing some other job that you were too busy to pick up my calls and even reply to my messages? And mom, dad! How could they not tell me that you were coming over! I would have at least made some preparations." He went on hugging and scolding me.

"Why, would you throw a party for my welcome?" I laughed.

"Yeah a grand party! And would have invited all species of monkeys and turtles! Now tell me why you didn't pick up my calls?"

"Don't you know I was mad at you? Should I make you remember what you did? Well, leave it. I don't want to." I pushed Kevin away and sat on the chair.

"Ashton, I would really appreciate if you could excuse us for a minute." Kevin said to Ashton, the person with whom Kevin shared his rented apartment, who was looking at us with his mouth open as if we are some animals who had run away from a zoo.

"Yeah dude, sure." People in London speak so softly that we Indians need pin drop silence to be able to hear them. Though Ashton wasn't one of them, but still spoke like them. He had come from Germany, and he too has got a scholarship for an engineering college.

"Tell me now, did you meet him again?" Kevin asked as Ashton left the house. "I wanted to, but he went somewhere." I replied as if I didn't want to have any conversation on this topic, showing absolutely no interest. I didn't want to remember that I ever met someone called Ayan.

"Went where?" Kevin investigated further. "Look I don't know, neither I want to. Just forget that there was a person named

Ayan ever in our lives, never ever mention him in front of me and focus on more important things of your life."

"Never expected to hear this from you. But I am glad." Kevin was surprised to see me so disinterested towards anything related to Ayan.

Later we chatted about everything. From even as silly things like how a rat eats to more important things like how my career choice changed. Soon after Ashton also joined us and started laughing and enjoying with us as if he has known us for years. It felt so nice to laugh and not keep my emotions just to myself after ages. It was so nice to have the feeling of not being alone. So nice to have a friend and so nice to have the satisfaction of never being betrayed, for why would my own brother leave me? I knew coming to London is a fresh start to everything. Even to my looks. My long-braided hair has changed to short burgundy coloured hair. My 'aunty like clothes' have changed to stylish ones, and my big glasses have become lenses. Kevin, Ashton and I went on talking for another few hours but I had to sleep early as the next day was a very big day for me. It was my interview at Oxford University.

***

"Wohooo! Party time! Party time! Yippeee!" I yelled as I reached home.

"You monkey, I am taking you back to the zoo and telling them to keep you under strict watch so that you never run away again." Kevin said in a sleepy voice. He had been studying the whole night so he completely forgot about my interview. "Leave me wherever you want to, but the people of Trinity College will bring me back!" I said dancing and jumping all around the house. "What! Did they select you?" Kevin asked disbelievingly.

"Yes! They did!"

We partied the whole night. Finally, I was going to study in abundance about my favourite thing and am on the walk of fulfilling my dreams. The next day was my first day in the college for which I was really excited. I didn't have much difficulty in adjusting. Not as I expected, people are very kind hearted here but as we know, exceptions are always there. But being there really helped me to forget my past. Coming to the university, it is like a heaven on earth. Jesus! I had seen so many big and beautiful buildings in Mumbai too, but it is like a seven-star resort, so big that you may even get lost. The sight of the beautiful gardens, pianos, and various other instruments made my eyes as wide as saucers. I can't even put that atmosphere into words.

The relationships between the students and the academic staff are so open and friendly that we almost forgot that we were studying. Their way of teaching helped me realize that studies can be actually fun sometimes. I had even become an active member of the orchestral group. Soon after, I started my own YouTube channel. I was not yet sure about my singing so I didn't expect to gain much followers. But I was shocked to see such a huge amount of comments on my first video and it was because of them that I got motivated to continue it further.

2011

Two years had passed by and my life is what I'll call a humdinger. A miracle happened to me. I got a call from XL Recordings! Somehow, they got to know about my channel and went bonkers! They contacted my university this morning and asked them for my details. My life is like a rollercoaster. It keeps on taking me up and down, giving me shivers every moment. Everything happened so quickly that I didn't even realize when it all happened. They called me for auditions, but I never ever knew that I could be this nervous. My feet were shaking as I went and stood in front of the mic. And my voice trembled as I try to sing.

"Miss Martins! This isn't a joke going on in here. Stop wasting our time. Jeremy! Play the music again." I was really petrified when the music director scolded me. I tried singing again for the umpteenth time, but I was unable to do so.

“Thank you, Miss Martins. We understand there’s a huge difference between singing on a mic in front of everyone and singing with your face hidden at your house. You may leave now.” *No! I can’t miss this opportunity, just because of a stupid thing called fear. No!*

“Sir, one more chance please, I promise, this time nothing will go wrong.” I said in as polite voice as possible.

“This shall be the last one. Play the music Jeremy,” the director said sternly.

Keeping in mind that it was my last opportunity, I gathered my nerves and started singing. I recalled what Ayan said that there’s no thing called fear, it’s all in our mind. I sang in such a way that was unbelievable even for me. *Singing is the thing I love the most, no, I couldn’t have any fear for it.*

“Well, that was. Marvellous!” The director clapped his hands in joy.

“Thank you, sir.” I breathed a sigh of relief. But deep down I felt sad that the person who taught me such important lessons of life was not with me anymore, and then I realised no matter how much I tell myself, his space in my life can never ever be filled by anyone else.

“We’ll start the recording from tomorrow Aarika, congratulations on your new album.” The music director signed a contract with me and shook hands. God, all this was just unbelievable. I didn’t even care to take the bus and ran at the fastest speed I could to reach the apartment.

“Guess what Kevin! Your sister isn’t a monkey anymore but a singer. Wake up Kevin! Ashton, at least you don’t be like my brother! Wake up both of you!” I was among such great people, who are always sleeping. Wow.

“Stop dreaming Aarika. Let me sleep,” Kevin said sluggishly and pushed me away. I filled a mug with cold water and threw it on him and Ashton, the super successful old Indian way of waking sleepyheads up. Just like my grandma used to wake me up back there in India.

"What, are you insane?" They both shivered and started roaring. I couldn't help but start laughing.

"Look at this," I said, handing them the contract. After reading it Kevin literally jumped out of his bed and Ashton started dancing around the house. They both looked even happier than me. And I was just thinking about one person now. How could I not share my biggest happiness with him? He would have been the happiest, I bet. People take less than a day to forget their families and friends. But that friend to whom you talked about your first crush, the one with whom you sneaked out of the house for the first time, the one in front of whom you had no shame in crying, the one who was there when you went through the difficult age of transforming into an adult from a teen—is it ever possible to forget that one?

***

We pass our judgments on various songs so easily, but we know little about the hard work behind it. In the process of recording my song, I felt like giving up so many times, but I just couldn't let such a great blessing slip from my hands. It isn't that everything was served to me on a platter, but still every one didn't get the opportunity that I got. After two months, my song was released and now that it's been six months, it is still on almost everyone's mind. People are finding it unique and tweeting things like, in the world ruled by pop music, they hadn't heard such a touching voice since the old times. It became much more popular than I thought. I really wished Ayan and Mayra could see what they have made me into. Had it not been for them I may not have realized my actual talent and dreams. I may not have discovered the world, where I actually belonged. Ah! I was loving my life even more than I could describe in words. But how could I believe the fact that my life would go on without taking any twists and turns? Wouldn't it be too boring then?

2015
Don't talk
to strangers

Four years, it just seems like a drop of water in our river like big life. But I have seen my life transform completely in these four years. I have seen just a common city girl rise to the top of the world. I have changed into a confident and successful young lady from a shy and silly girl. The girl, who was even scared to sing in front of a few people in her school, is now singing in front of a thousand people in concerts. The singers, whom I used to admire so much, are now tweeting to appreciate me. The loner Aarika is now no longer alone and is always surrounded by lots and lots of fans. I made an acquaintance with some of the greatest singers whose guidance helped me so much and they have also started to invite me to their grand parties.

Everything became so royal for me. In my family nobody cared to click my pictures even when I begged them to do so but now the photographers didn't even want to miss a single chance to take my shots. Mom and dad were finally proud of my decision. One of the many good things that happened to me in these four years was Brooklyn Hart. From handling my worst breakups to making me laugh till my stomach hurts, she has done everything so beautifully for me.

Unlike my early teen years when I got worried when a new day started, I had now begun to wait eagerly and excitedly to see what each day has in store for me. I had been on a tour for my concerts in different cities and countries for the past one month and witnessed some of the most beautiful views. It made me happy and saddened me at the same time that Italy was the second last city I would be performing in. I missed Kevin and Brooke, but I didn't want to stop travelling.

***

Once you are in this industry, you can't hide a single flaw from the camera. So, I had been extra concerned about my looks and figure and thus working out in the gym had become an integral part of my day. So as usual I went to the gym in the hotel, when mystery came knocking at my door.

"Excuse me, it seems you have dropped something."

Ayan! Was he back? The voice was same as Ayan's voice. Even if any difference was there then it was so slight that nobody could point it out. I looked back and saw my room key lying on the floor. He too had turned back and I couldn't see his face, but his structure also looked exactly the same, except his straight and a bit longer hair.

"Thank you so much!" Hearing my voice, he turned towards me.

"You're welcome." It wasn't Ayan, his face was entirely different and he replied so normally as if I am just an ordinary person for him. He was as white as milk. He had devilish looks, yet he was very attractive. It was like an entire world of sin lived in his eyes, but a whole universe of charm resided in his body. He had various wounds on his face and hands, some fresh, some old. His eyes were as blue as an ocean; he is what you'll call stunning.

He looked so similar to Ayan and that made me want to watch him more and more. Even though I wanted to leave I just couldn't. Everything about him was just too captivating for my will to fight. I just wanted to hear his voice for as long as possible. In these six years I always told myself that I hated Ayan. But a best friend is someone who is the hardest to hate. Ayan had left an unforgettable mark on my heart and no matter what I did I could never forget him. "You won't ask for an autograph, huh?" I asked jocularly to start a conversation.

"Why would I want someone's autograph whom I've just met?" He replied as if he seriously had no clue about who I was.

"You seriously refuse to know Aarika Martins?"

"Who said that I don't know you? But that doesn't mean that I'll run after you, begging for your autograph."

"Strange, now let's rush to the breakfast hall. If we don't hurry up, we'll miss the delicious breakfast" I laughed. He was weird. Really, really weird.

"You are 'The Aarika Martins', don't they have any special arrangement for your grand breakfast in your own room?"

"They had, but I refused to take it. I prefer to have my meals with my fans." I tried to keep the conversation light.

"Oh, shut up! Crying on the stage doesn't make anyone as popular as you think you are. To be honest I didn't even remember your name clearly until you introduced yourself." I tried to take it as a humorous reply, but deep inside I knew that he didn't intend to sound humorous. Had it been anyone else I would have slapped him, but nothing he said sounded bad to me. His voice reminded me of someone I really loved.

"If you know it not then what you are calling 'crying' is actually singing high pitch songs. What's your name by the way?"

"Samar Malhotra. Are you going to sit with me?" He asked as if he is a prince or something; his standards are very high and he saw me as a girl of inferior birth whom he doesn't want to sit with.

"I'll not if you don't want to."

"I don't want anything. You can do as you wish." I didn't get exactly what he was saying, but as far as I could make out, it was that he wasn't in too much favour of me sharing a table with him. But even after hearing and seeing everything, I couldn't go away and like an idiot, I sat down with him.

"So, what do you do?" I asked.

"Not torture people with my singing because I know I can't sing. Why don't you do the same? Besides I am a lawyer too." Had it been any normal person, he would have felt like the luckiest person on this earth for having such a famous singer sit with him and that too when he didn't ask me to do so, and had not behaved very nicely with me. But he, he was replying just for the sake of replying, all his attention was stuck in his phone and food. And his first comment was so rude, but still I ignored it. The only reason why I was tolerating this nonsense was because he made me feel Ayan's presence around me. I can stand anyone but not people who are full of pride.

"Oh great! You know there was a time when I had my mind motivated for the legal profession, but then destiny."

"Trust me, you wouldn't have even gotten into any respectable university of law. You can do nothing else except crying on the stage." I don't think he had any idea of what he was saying as he was too busy in relishing his food.

"Excuse me? I was capable of that also, but I would have never got the pleasure and satisfaction that I get now."

"Being surrounded by people always gives you pleasure? Poor you. I wish I could show you what actual pleasure is but I am too busy to waste my time on you."

"Ma'am may we have your autograph?" First two people came, seeing them a bunch of people also gather around the table.

"What autograph!? Who is she? Is she your God? Or you guys had nothing to do so you came to waste your time here? You beggars go beg somewhere else. Bloody losers." Then it was enough! He had crossed all his limits!

"Excuse me Mr. Samar, I have had enough of your nonsense. Till now I was tolerating you just because you reminded me of someone really close to my heart. You've been going on and on for the past one hour and I took it all as a joke. But dare you say anything to these innocent people! And here's a gift for you." I gave him a slap and threw the glass of water on his face. Tears welled in my eyes. No one had ever hurt me to this extent. I couldn't help but cry. Unfortunately, a reporter recorded the whole episode and posted it on the net. It is difficult to give an account of all the ignominy faced by me. I felt that I was really bad at choosing the right people. I decided to forget the whole thing and concentrate on the concert. And also, I had something better to look forward to that night as many Indians were staying in the hotel, so the manager of this hotel, being an Indian has organized Ghazal Nights.

After a tiring, yet a beautiful day I came back to the hotel and got ready. It was really good to see everyone dressed in an Indian attire in a foreign land. People were coming on the stage and reciting shayaris, some written by them, some by age-old famous poets like Mirza Ghalib. “A round of applause for Riya Khanna. We’ll have Arjun next with a beautiful and one of the best shayaris about love by the one of the greatest poets. It’s now time for a short break, enjoy the evening.”

“Kitni awaazein hain, yeh log hain, baatein hai magar zehan ke peeche kisi aur hi sataha pe kahin jaise chupchaap barasta tasavvur tera.”

When they talked about shayaris on love, this was the first one that comes to my mind. I was so excited that I didn’t even realise that I said these words aloud and just then I heard a voice from behind.

“Your gentle tears fell on my heart in such a way that it blossomed all the flowers and joined the numerous pieces of my heart lying apart. Your reproachful eyes have so much power that it made the heart to feel again that was for so long sour. I fail to understand my eyes that always abhorred you, how have they started to adore you? But it lustily cries that it gave you so much worry, from the bottom of my heart I want to said sorry.”

I turned back and saw it was the same arrogant guy, Samar. “Oh God! Stop speaking Mr. Malhotra or my ears shall start bleeding. Move away.” I picked my things and started heading towards another table for I couldn’t even tolerate the shadow of that man around me now. Even though he crazily reminded me of Ayan, I just didn’t want to see his face. “Oh, I know as much as I love listening to shayaris and poems, I suck at composing them.” He laughed and blushed. I didn’t know that even he knew how to smile. “You? You like poetry? You know, you have to have emotions to understand and feel the very essence of poetry, which you definitely lack.”

“I always used to listen to Ghazals with my dad. He loved it. These Ghazals are the only memory of his left with me.” His usual arrogant tone had turned to that of pain now. And all of a sudden, I felt guilty for being so rude.

"Uh I am really sorry." I said, all awkward by now.

"I am sorry too." He said smiling. We talked for a while and I felt as if I had already known him for a long, long time now. He told me all about himself and I, all about myself. There was something about him that was weird. Normal people don't behave like him, yet he was the most charming person I had ever come across. I felt as if I would find a good friend in him.

"You aren't as bad as I thought," I told him.

"Oh dear, I am worse," he said with a wide grin on his face. I never imagined that I could get on so well with a person like him and finally it felt all the unpleasantness I faced in the morning was worth it.

"Apart from singing, what makes you happy?" He asked, grabbing a drink and making himself comfortable on the chair beside me.

"Making others happy," I said without taking more than a second to think.

"Weird," He said with a frown, but then started smiling. He had a very hesitant smile. It was almost as if he didn't know how to smile at all. "Want to go out? The weather is lovely." I looked at him with surprise when he said this.

"Tell me honestly, are you even a human? How can you call such a chilly weather lovely?"

"Are you kidding me? What's better than a combination of an ice cream, long walks, and a biting cold wind. It's the perfect adventure, come on." He dragged me out of my chair.

"God, why do I come across adventure lovers always! Anyway, if you insist, I am ready to give it a try." It was so cold outside that we were barely able to speak. We walked among the howling winds and whistling petals of the flowers in the garden.

They had a unique and a beautiful arrangement of fairy lights there.

"So, where do you live?" I asked, wearing a jacket. I was already wearing three to four pieces of clothing, so this should be a fair idea of where I stood at that moment. I looked like a panda who was unable to carry the weight of its own body.

"Kensington 8, London."

"Oh my God, I live in Knightsbridge SW7!" We both were amazed at how close we lived. This gave us more and more topics to talk about. We talked for hours until I realized it was almost 1 a.m. I was laughing my heart off the whole time, though the guy didn't know how to laugh much, but he sure had got an appreciable sense of humour.

"I am going to take off now, big day tomorrow. By the way, do you mind telling me why you have so many wounds on your face? Why everything about you is so distorted? Your phone's screen is broken, your hands are bruised. More than a lawyer you seem like a street fighter. Why?" As I said this, the muscle above his right eye started twitching. He closed his eyes and took a long breath. He smashed the glass of drink in his hands.

"Just. Just mind your own bloody business. Don't try to know more than what is being told to you." He held both my hands so tightly that he was almost hurting me, with his eyes wide open.

"Okay. Okay I am sorry. Good night. Sleep well." All frightened by now, I moved away from him and left. In fact, I almost ran back to my room. This guy wasn't normal, and I didn't want any further interactions with him. Samar was the other name for trouble. I regretted exchanging phone numbers with him. I shouldn't have pitied such a beast. I shouldn't trust people so easily. God, I am so dumb.

The next two days I saw him several times, but avoided him. He tried calling my name but I didn't stop. Being with a person like him was equivalent to risking your life.

"Samar, just leave me alone. I can't tell you how sorry I feel for you. If you think acting like this makes you look cooler, then it doesn't. You need some help. Be with good people, help others, I don't know what, but do something good in life. All the best. May a great future lie ahead. It was nice meeting you. Goodbye."

***

The streets of London were enlivened with the Christmas spirit. It is impossible not to enjoy the merriment flowing in each and every nook of London during Christmas. Christmas is also an occasion for all the big shots to make a grandeur display of their possessions, so one can get to witness some of the best parties on this day. My way of spending Christmas has been simple and exactly the same since I was a kid. I start my day by playing Christmas songs on my grandmother's old-fashioned radio. It was her much beloved chattel and so was I. Hence, out of all her kids and grandkids, she chose to give it to me before dying. Much to my surprise, with a little bit of servicing it works perfectly even today.

After putting on my new clothes I go to the church for carol singing and wallow in the heavenly ditties all around me. Then usually I have got somewhere to perform for Christmas, so that takes another hour of my day. After that, me and Brooklyn dress up as Santas and go to distribute gifts among the orphans and other kids in the city followed by dinner at Joe-Joe's. Not very posh, it's a small place but has the most amazing food and a remarkably good collection of music. There's something beautiful about its aura. In the evening it feels like the best relaxing place and by the night gives you enough energy to dance your heart out. Exactly the kind of place Brooke and I enjoy being in. Sometimes, other friends or our boyfriends join us too. *Well that happened ages ago, we both have been single for a remarkably long while now. Who would want to date a lunatic and then also tolerate her lunatic best friend?* But most often it's just Brooklyn and me.

She is probably the only girl in London who doesn't judge me for my craziness but makes me do even crazier things. She's an amazing photographer and even a better artist. I met her in an art exhibition a few years back. In fact, many of my house's walls have been decorated by her paintings. She is just as twisted as her perfect curls falling on to her shoulders, but her heart as captivating and beautiful as her eyes. Kevin mocks us that always it's just Brooklyn and me, but he is unaware of the fun we have, which may not have been possible with anyone else's company without being judged. Somehow, we never get bored in each other's company.

Coming back to my schedule, then we both go to Berkeley's rooftop theatre followed by sluggish mumblings about how grateful we are for this life and super philosophical talk. Today I'll be performing at Arena 02, for which I had been excited for weeks. It's not like the normal concerts, there's just something different about the Christmas Spirit!

***

After performing at Arena 02, Brooke and I went to the Abode of Hope. That's actually my favourite part of Christmas. Brooke had actually dressed as a Santa. Apart from the regular clothes, she had put on a white beard and even put a lot of paper balls inside her clothes which made her look super funny and super fat.

"How does my tummy look? You gotta admit, I look hot!" she said rubbing her stomach and putting on the cap.

"Why don't I see any difference? Aren't you this fat always?" I said punching her belly. One of the balls fell out. She too almost fell down. She was looking way too hilarious.

As we went inside, the mere sight of Brooke was enough to arouse everyone's laughter and spirit of enjoyment. Brooke showed her weird Santa dance and I sang and played violin for them.

"Whoa Aarika, seems like you got a new date. I have been observing him for a while now, he can't get his eyes off of you. Oh my God I am jealous, he is too hot for this world." Brooke said in an overdramatic manner, acting to fan her face with her hand. I was unable to see the guy as many people had gathered around him, they were playing a game or something.

"Wait, isn't that Samar Malhotra? The attorney for Mark Linetski, that Italian guy case? I read an article about him, he's been in the news quite a lot for some days now. Whoa! That case still gives me shivers." As Brooke took that horrid name, I could feel goosebumps on my arm. I had not yet forgotten what all he did in Italy. And as I went forward, I saw a startling sight. I saw that devilish, yet charming smile among those innocent kids. He was playing with them cheerfully, for once talking to people like humans. I did not want to face him, so I planned to leave. But that fathead Brooklyn had vanished all of a sudden. I spotted her then removing her beard and taking out her paper balls.

"Hello Aarika, Merry Christmas!" When I was watching Brooke, I heard a whisper in my ear. That voice sent shivers down my spine. My heart started beating faster. I felt something in the pit of my stomach. I knew it was not Ayan, but with that voice I could almost feel him around me. I turned around and found that it was Samar. I don't know why I mistake his voice for Ayan's, always. Memories of the night in Italy make him look attractive, but side by side super scary. But what I saw him doing today had nullified the effect.

"Hello, Samar. Merry Christmas to you too. It was great seeing what you were doing out there. Behaving like that makes you look human. You should do it more often."

"Oh my God! You both actually know each other! He was not making stuff up! Oh my God ma'am I am like your biggest fan in entire London. Not just for your singing but what you did to this guy. You just took a few hours to do what his uncle, aunt, and I had been trying to do for years! You made him do humane things. He can't stop smiling and singing since he got back from

Italy. He has been talking about you all day and all night. And Abode of Hope! It's the last place where you could imagine the old Samar. Oh my God, I am hyperventilating. I am Flynn Lester, by the way. Hello to you too, cute Santa." All that he said was just too hard to digest. I couldn't believe that someone like Samar could have friends too. The guy's super crazy and over excited. He was speaking so fast that he almost skipped two-three words in between.

"Well Samar, that's impressive. I couldn't have gotten a better Christmas gift than knowing that you have changed so much overnight. Keep up the good work. See you around maybe, got to go right now. Brooklyn and I have some plans," I said dragging Brooke along. But she left my hand and stopped.

"Aarika didn't give me time to introduce myself. I am Brooklyn Hart. Nice to meet you both!" She shook hands with Samar and then with Flynn. But her handshake with Flynn lasted for an eternity. They both couldn't stop blushing and looking at each other.

"Brooke, aren't we getting late?" I said in my please-save-me-Brooke voice, but for the first time in so many years she didn't recognize it.

"Why don't you guys join us?" Samar came and asked me. I didn't even reply anything, but just looked at him with my reproachful eyes.

"Look Aarika, I messed up that night. But believe me, I have changed a lot since then. Each word that you said has managed to occupy some or the other corner of my heart. I want to apologize for that night. Won't you give another chance to this friendship, one last chance?" Whoa! Samar Malhotra knows how to apologize? That was some brand-new information for me.

"Aarika Martins, it's not just one hot guy, it's two. I think we both are getting dates tonight! We do social work every Christmas, we are being paid for it this time." Brooke came and whispered in my ear.

"Of course, she will, Aarika Martins has a very big heart." Brooke told Samar and Flynn without even asking me. Oh, this girl is mad. But after thinking it for a while, I gave my approval to it. Forgiveness is a divine virtue, isn't that what I have learnt since I was five?

***

Brooke had been laughing at Flynn's jokes straight for three hours now. I knew that douche was going to complain that her jaws hurt badly when we got back home. There had been an awkward silence between me and Samar, accompanied by exchange of formal smiles. He indeed has changed a lot and started to make a display of his gentlemanliness. He pulled out chairs for us, opened the car doors, spoke softly, and even better, didn't speak nonsense. I really wish we were at the Joe-Joe's back then, but there I was stuck at a very grand, yet boring restaurant. Everyone was just eating there with utter sophistication and smiling for the sake of smiling. There was a deafening silence. Had I brought Brooke to this place, she wouldn't have stayed for a minute, but now she didn't care about anything. Everything for her except Flynn, seemed to have faded.

"Aarika, I am sorry. I know I can be angry sometimes, but that day I had crossed my limits. I was really disturbed and upset that day. And guys like me use anger to hide their desolation. They are too proud to lay bare their sadness. I don't even know how to make it up to you." Samar was entirely a different man than whom I met in Italy. I really hoped these were not just pretentions.

"I know my act is unforgivable and you still hate me. But Aarika Martins, isn't hatred the beginning of some of the best love stories?" He looked straight into my eyes with his same devilish smile.

He kept apologizing for almost an hour and later revealed that it was his father's death anniversary that day, and there was another reason which he couldn't share with me. I didn't force him, for after all his warnings during our previous meeting I did not want to know him more than what he wanted me to.

But I won't deny, once we started talking, I had a marvellous time. We all did.

That night four people, mad in their own ways, and completely different from each other, had become friends. And some more than just friends. That night was the start to some of the best moments of our lives and many more that we were yet to witness.

2015
Don't drink
too much

"Is the world square or is the world round? Am I in the sky or on the ground? How many drinks did I have, did anyone count?"

No! Don't you think that I am that spoilt girl who gets drunk and starts saying rubbish things. I had never crossed my limits or for that matter never even touched alcohol, but today the atmosphere forced me to do so. It had been a long time since I had come back from the tour and I had been working day and night. I desperately needed a break and my pop star friend, Bianca's birthday party offered me the perfect break. But I had forgotten that her party too would be extra royal like her, where you have to sit with respect, eat with respect, and if boredom is killing you, then die with respect. Such royalty was way too much for me to handle. Nobody cared if I hid myself in some corner but if I left, I would have been asked a thousand questions to which I had no answers.

"Madam would you like to have anything?" The waiter asked. I didn't even realise in which corner I went as I was really busy in reading and replying to my fan emails since I hadn't gotten time for that lately. Every seat was occupied or even if it wasn't, someone known was sitting there and I was already very tired so I wanted to spend some alone time. "Whatever you'll like to give sir. Something good and put a lot of ice in it. I feel really suffocated."

I smiled and then comforted myself on a chair behind the waiter where no one could see me. "Here you go ma'am." The waiter said handing me a glass. I thought it was just a normal soft drink but once I tasted it, it seemed like the best drink ever.

"Can I have another glass of this please?"

"Yeah sure ma'am but the place you are sitting in isn't meant for you. It's for the staff."

"You don't instruct me," I laughed.

I didn't even realise how many glasses I drank and how much I had eaten while going through the mails, it was so…so lovely to see how much they loved me. After I finished reading those I started going through my old snaps and stuffing myself with more and more food and drinks. Among all other messages, I saw Samar's message. "Hey Aarika, been a long time. Meet soon!" In another one hour I had totally lost control of myself and started murmuring weird things to myself. I felt as if I was the only thing still and rest everything was shaking. My eyes were droopy, but still I managed to get up. And that's what made me realise that I had gone to the hard drinks' counter.

"Hello Jess! Where were you!? I was searching for you!" I am such a good liar. I saw Jess, my once upon a time very good friend, who had completely forgotten me, at least a thousand times, but didn't care to say hello to her. But by this time, I myself had no idea of what I wanted and what I was doing.

"Oh darling, I was also looking for you. Uh you don't look so good. Are you all right?" I was dancing without the music. Numerous types of music were playing in my mind which made me step on someone's feet, table cloths, someone's dresses and finally on Jess' new best friend Julianne. "Did you just step on my Jimmy Choo heels!? How dare you!" Julianne yelled at me as I stepped on her 'expensive heels' and dropped the drink in my hand. To be honest, I wouldn't have taken those heels even if someone offered them to me for free.

"Oh yes I did. You didn't see? Should I step again?" I talked to her with such courtesy that it made her even madder than before.

"You moron!" Julianne was also saying some courteous words but Jess pushed her back.

"Aarika, you are not okay. Come with me." Jess held my hand and took me outside the hotel.

"Now tell me, what's wrong with you? Do you have any idea what you did inside?" Jess scolded me.

"You own a private jet, right?" I changed the topic, trying to control my balance.

"Yes, but that's not the answer to my question. I asked what's wrong with you."

"Rich people huh? Oh, wait what is that shiny thing? Let me have a look," I said bending down and pointing to her sparkling sandals, and removing them from her feet causing her to trip badly. Had anyone seen her expression they would have died laughing.

"I am just tired of you Aarika, please cut it out! Here I am putting so much effort to help you and there you are making me fall. You know what? You should be in a mental asylum and not here. Just go away!"

"And probably you need to be there more than me. You bitch!" I screamed. But she was too infuriated, and walked away without saying anything. She didn't say anything to me, but God knows what a long list of bad words would have been made for me that day by her. I sat in the middle of the garden laughing at my own jokes. That day I finally got to know why our elders curse mobile phones so much. Just because of my absent mindedness I landed in so many troubles. But it didn't get over there. A lot more was yet to come.

"Hello David! How are you doing?" I couldn't believe I talked so nicely to my chauffeur for the first time. Though I have always been very compassionate to all my servants and drivers, but David wasn't one of them. He is a tall man with fiery eyes, fierce voice, and rude behaviour but also, he is very trustworthy and hardworking.

"I think I am doing fine ma'am, but you don't look so well."

"Unenthusiastic people like you often fail in judging happy people correctly. Now take me to this address." I said, handing him my phone while sitting in the car.

"Oh David, what an intelligent person you are! Built a home for yourself in this luxurious car. Nail cutter, PSP, blankets, beer bottles, cold drinks, chips, um, what else do we have… Oh, I love this comb David! What a brainy boy you are!" Had it been any normal day I would have scolded him for misusing my car, but it was his lucky day so he got saved.

"What else would I do huh? When you'll all of a sudden make plans to stay overnight or behave as if you've not kept anyone waiting in the car, I'll also need some entertainment, wouldn't I?" He replied as if I'd hurt his ego and he would kill me for that.

"Oh, I thought that is what I used to pay you for. Let me also make some use of these luxuries today." I took his blanket, wrapped it around my body and got down from the car.

"Hello?" I rang the doorbell.

"Yes? How can I help you?" An almost bald man, finding it so hard to not let his eyes shut, opened the door.

"Hello sir, can I see Samar?" I was so sleepy that my voice sounded like that of an old man.

"May I know what your urgency is that you want to see Samar at 3 in the morning? And why the hell are you carrying this fatuous blanket with you?" He looked at me as if he was doing the most important task of his life and I snatched the opportunity from him. Well sleep, in today's life is one such opportunity that is available to all but only a few lucky ones get enough of it. When I myself forgot the reason for going at Samar's place and was unable to answer, he pulled the blanket from my face.

"Oh my God! Aarika Martins! I am so sorry, please come in." The expression of resentment on his face turned into an expression of guilt.

"Thank you so much sir!"

"Samar's room is upstairs, you'll have to make a lot of effort to wake him up, he is a big sleepyhead." he laughed.

"Okay sir. And thank you again." Somehow tripping and dancing I reached Samar's room. While sleeping his face looked as innocent as a lamb and nobody could ever judge what devil he actually was. There was a small grin on his face which normally appeared once in a blue moon. The cool breeze coming from his window was slowly raising his hair upwards. I found it so unusual to see him so calm, and for a change smiling. I put all my hair on my face and yelled in his ear to scare him.

"Move away! I swear I'll shoot you. I have a gun!" I didn't think of this to happen. I thought he'd be scared. But I was wrong. Samar wasn't a man whom you could frighten. But he was a man who even scared the thieves away.

"Relax Samar, it's me. Only you don't have the right to frighten others." I said, laughing. I thought he would scream at me, hit me, throw me out of his house, but today none of the above things happened, which finally made me stop giggling.

"Aarika, you, it's so good to see you after so long. Uh please have a seat." His voice calmed down. He blushed a little and scratched his head. There was some hesitation in his voice as if he was trying to hide something.

"I see you have a very beautiful garden, do you mind going there?" The night was all calm, peaceful, and starry, so I was craving to go out.

"But you'll fall sick, it's so chilly outside." he said rubbing his eyes.

"Wasn't it you who said, 'What's better than a combination of an ice cream, long walks, and a biting cold wind. It's the perfect adventure. Blabla...'"

"Honestly tell me, are you drunk?" he asked as we lay on the grass and watched the stars. Words are less to describe the beauty of the tranquillity at that moment. I had never felt the way I was feeling that night; as if the whole world had come to rest, and Samar and I were the only alive souls on the face of Earth.

"Let's not ruin the moment by talking about that. Samar, my life has become full of noise. This is not the kind of life I dreamt of. I know I love my life, but just for a short period I feel like escaping the world of reality and hiding myself in some peaceful spot. Don't you think in this noise we are slowly losing our joy and that we desperately need a break?" I asked watching the stars and realizing that how much I was in need of some more calm time like this.

"I agree, let's plan a trip to some serene place. Even I feel like getting away with the daily routine for a few days. How about Kashmir? We'll get to show Brooke and Flynn our country, and Kashmir is famous for its serenity. All our purposes will be fulfilled and also I want to meet your parents."

"Perfect then. By the way it was rea—really nice of your Dad to let me come in so late at night." I had become even droopier than before. I was barely able to speak.

"He's not my dad. He's my uncle. Don't you remember I told you about dad?" His voice became despondent as he sank into a pool of thoughts.

"Where's your mom and dad then?" Had I been in my right senses I would have never said that thing, but it was very silly of me at that time to not understand that the mention of his parents made him sad.

"I don't know about mom. I last met her almost fifteen years ago, when I was thirteen. Now I have no idea where she is."

"And may I know why?" I had become child-like, going on asking questions without even realizing the impact of it on the other person.

"You won't understand. Nobody has broken your heart yet."

"What! You are saying that I won't understand how it feels to have your heart broken by your loved ones? Oh, dear boy you are mistaken." I started laughing. But my laughter was the one in which immense pain was hidden and then I narrated the whole story of what happened between me, Ayan, and Kevin.

"You know I used to think that there's no one in this world who'll ever love me or there's no one whom I'll ever be able to love. But since the day I met you my thinking changed, I changed. My bitter heart melted. You made me feel again the feeling I thought, I thought that never existed. But I can't believe how hard I have fallen for you." No wonder why he was the way he was. Behind every such uncouth behaviour, there is a hidden story which we often tend to ignore. What all he said was going above my head. All I could see was some spiral sort of things in front of my eyes, and all I could hear was the echo of the tunes that I hummed.

"Aarika, are you awake?" He said moving hair from my face as my eyes gently closed.

"Yeah," I said in a soft voice.

"I know I am not worth it, but still I want you to know that everything may come to an end. But not my love. My love for you is going to be forever." If the normal Aarika would have heard it all she would have been stunned, but the drunken Aarika childishly made fun of him.

"First you tell me, how long is going to be your forever? Five months, five weeks or five days? You know, Jason Parker? He said that he is going to be by my side forever. He broke up with me after two weeks and now I don't know even know where he is." I laughed.

"When I say something, I mean it. I have not heard of any more stupid person than Jason. You are so unique that it only requires the thought of your presence to make me feel better. I thought you'd be rude like other superstars. You don't care all the time about how you look. I know you'll have no shame in going out in your elephant print pyjamas in front of everyone. You are carefree. You are different, not only from the superstars, but from each and every person on this earth. This makes me love you more and more. This makes me want more and more to run away with you and establish my own world with just you in it. I cherish you above everything else in my life. I don't know the extent of Jason's idiocrasy but it must be great for how can anyone leave a person like you? I know you are a great singer and a person like me is not worthy to be in your life but I want you to know that I … I am in love with you." What! Love! Is he the same person who once called me the most monotonous person alive, or is he the same person who didn't even want to share his table with me for breakfast?

"With all my heart I want to tell you that nobody can love you the way I do." He said it again when I didn't reply the first time. His voice became more intense this time.

"Oh nice." I didn't understand what was being said to me and still I said such a stupid thing and soon after, fell asleep. I tried hard to remember what happened after that, but I was unable to do so.

***

The next morning, I woke up with a light head and noticed a blanket over me. Something dropped at the tip of my nose; I thought it was snowing again. But when I saw what actually it was, my throat collapsed, my breath stopped for a second. It was blood. I saw Samar looking right into my eyes, smiling, with his fingers stuck to the tip of the knife, bleeding. I realized then that I had been sleeping the whole night in Samar's garden only.

"Good morning, sweetheart. Slept well?" He asked with a grin on his face.

"Samar, what's that knife for? What are you doing with it?" I somehow tried to get words out of my frozen mouth, frozen both because of cold and fear.

"Oh, I brought an apple for you. Should I cut it? You must be feeling hungry." When he fetched an apple, which was kept behind him, I got a sense of relief that it was just the apple he wanted to cut and nothing else.

Hearing his usual harsh words turn into sweet ones, I got up and recollected what all had happened the other night. Recollecting what all I had done, I became a bundle of nerves. I was too panicky to say anything, so I ran away without saying anything. He kept calling me and running after me, but I ran faster. I was ashamed. Ashamed of everything I said and everything I did. I had already texted Brooklyn. She must be here anytime.

"Someone said she never drinks?" Brooke taunted me; I could tell she was mad at me.

"I did not do it intentionally; it was a mistake, okay?" I said in my defence.

"And then landing at Samar's place was a mistake too?" her soft voice grew a little louder.

"I was too drunk to think sensibly, I am sorry, okay?"

"Stop yelling! By the way, me and Flynn had one heck of a night yesterday. He was wearing a black shirt with his sleeves rolled up and black trousers, which of course he did to impress me. And guess what, I am impressed! He is so hot! His veins were so prominent and oh God I looked at his eyes for the first time so closely. They are greener than an emerald. I couldn't stop laughing the whole night. Forgive me, but he is even funnier than you. But after that we didn't mind having a little romantic and philosophical talk. I won't tell you that of course, it's embarrassing, and also other stuff too that's even more embarrassing. Just because of your message I had to bid him adieu. He left me saying, 'Brooklyn Hart, you have stolen my heart!' Can you believe how lame that was, but God it drove me crazy! He drives me crazy! I have gone bonkers! Help me!" She was blushing so profusely and speaking quickly. She only does that when she really happy or nervous. And I could see that she was both happy and nervous at that time. I wondered what all happened the previous night.

"You spent the whole night with Flynn Lester! Had we all lost our minds yesterday? Are you two secretly dating!" I said, pretending to be angry, which of course, I was not.

"We aren't dating or anything okay? We both just wanted to know each other better, which we won't be able to do with two boring people around." She calmed down a bit and started laughing.

"Now that you've found a guy, of course you're going to find me boring." I made a sad face.

On the way back, I left these messages to Samar:

"Samar I am so sorry for what all happened yesterday. I wasn't in my right senses."

"I shouldn't have come to your house this way."

Samar: "Why are you apologizing? It was a privilege to have you at my home. But yes, you shouldn't have left that way. I wanted to spend some more time with you. Had a great time last night. Keep giving such surprises. By the way, is the Kashmir thing still on?" He replied instantly. I was so relaxed to see that he was behaving normally.

"Yeah, for sure. Book the tickets and let's get done with visa formalities and all as soon as possible." I felt that this trip would be a good opportunity to get away with the awkwardness between us.

"See you at your place at 8. Okay?" he asked.

"Okay."

***

We had dinner together and decided everything regarding the trip. Samar didn't mention anything he said the other day. It was a four-day trip. We planned to leave London after two days and decided to stay in a tree house.

"See you tomorrow," Samar said and left. I was again alone with my thoughts. I felt as if my life had suddenly changed and I was completely helpless. Nothing was the same. However, I decided to forget everything and indulge myself in packing for the trip as it was a great thing to help me to overcome my embarrassment. I first decided to talk about all this to Kevin, but later felt that he may tell mom and dad as well, though he would never do that, but still I thought it wasn't wise. After all it's better to keep some things to yourself only.

***

We didn't even realise when we reached Kashmir. Though the journey was very long, Samar's jokes made it feel really short. I was completely unaware of the other side which existed in him that was caring, funny, and knew how to laugh. During the twelve hours of flight none of us closed our eyes even once, and it was the time when our friendship became even stronger. I was laughing my heart out. It felt as if I had known him for years, but who knew how wrong I was.

"Hello mom! Guess where I am?" I surprised mom by calling her early in the morning.

"Where are you honey?" her voice seemed as if she was in a deep sleep.

"I am in Kashmir!" I said excitedly.

"Oh great, this time if you go back without coming to Mumbai, you'll get a nice one from me." Even in half sleep she scolded me. This is the thing that is the most special about mothers. They don't fail to show their love in any circumstances.

"I am not coming over. You and dad have to be here at any cost as soon as possible. I am here for just four days. Get up and go book the tickets."

"All right, all right. We'll be there."

"Promise?"

"Anything for our darling daughter." She gave a kiss on the phone and then disconnected the call.

***

I was so busy in feeling the fresh and cold breeze of Kashmir that I didn't even realise when my foot twisted and I fell down. It was nothing unusual for me as I keep bumping into things and falling, always.

"Oh my God, Aarika! Are you fine? No, it's all my mistake. I wasn't taking care of you. Had I held your hand you wouldn't have fallen down. I have to be punished for this." Before I could say anything, he moved towards a car and started hitting his hand really hard. My mouth was left wide open. He did that for five continuous minutes, until I went and stopped him. I had begun to feel afraid now. Was I hanging out with some psycho? It really scared the shit out of me. I hadn't seen anyone do such weird things before.

***

We first planned to go to the tree house in Srinagar and then leave for the city tour. The air was so cold and fresh. It was so exciting to be back in the country after so long and that too to a place where no one recognized me except for some tourists who came from big cities where English music was popular. It was the month of November, so it was snowing, and that added to the beauty of the place. I had never seen such greenery anywhere. The snow-covered tips of the green leaves were looking so lovely that I was forced to capture it. The people there in the *phirans* were looking adorable. The light music that the driver played added to the beauty of the atmosphere. But Samar's presence scared me. Every time I was with him he gave me a new reason to be surprised.

"Ain't everything so beautiful?" Samar asked searching for something in his bag.

"Yes, beyond one's imagination." There was a bit hesitation in my voice as I was still shaken from what he did.

"Take this," he said handing me a bunch of keys.

"What's this?

"The spare keys of my house. I want you to be as safe as possible. Whenever you are in any need or just feel like coming even at four in the morning, just use these."

"Thank you so much!" It was unbelievable that a person like Samar could care so much for someone. Maybe this is what the spirit of love does. It changes Satan like people to angels. We were engulfed in euphoria until we got obstructed by the traffic jam. Little did we know that a petty traffic jam would become a big life threat? The beautiful music that the driver played soon changed to melancholic one. The driver's eyes became red and watery.

"What's wrong with him?" Samar and I said at the same time.

The driver opened the window, moved his head out, and started murmuring things to himself. He made funny faces and said absurd things in some other language which we couldn't understand. Tears were rolling down his cheeks. Then he started doing some weird dance moves with his hands. We instantly got to know that he was mentally sick. After another fifteen-twenty minutes, the jam cleared and that was when the trouble began. The policeman and the driver were at each other's throats as the driver wasn't moving his taxi forward and misbehaving on the road. Samar insisted on driving, but the driver was too attached with his damaged car to let anyone else drive. The argument with the policeman grew hotter and as a result the driver threw a glass bottle on the policeman and drove at the maximum speed.

"Hello sir! What are you doing? Are you in your right senses? Stop the car and let us get down!" Samar yelped at the driver.

"I am just taking to you places where you can't go on your own, forget about getting down and even if you do where would you go?" That was the main thing. Where would we go? Being in a completely different place is equivalent to being on a different planet. We didn't even know a single thing about the place. But at least if we got down we could find some way out, because then we would be alive to think.

"Please stop the car!" Samar and I yelled. But that didn't make any difference. He took the car on undeveloped roads and drove on the edges from where if we would fall, we would directly go to heaven. The car was going zigzag-zigzag, which made my head shake more than the time I was drunk. The radio in the car stopped working, but we didn't feel its absence at all, as the driver was going on telling us anecdotes from his childhood; how he was betrayed by numerous people in his life — and then he started singing plaintive songs. This was going on until the driver tried taking the car on a snow-covered hill and it stopped working. That was just the golden moment for us to save our lives. We took all our things and ran even faster than Usain Bolt and reached the top of the hill with much effort. Why the driver did that was still a mystery. He was probably too drunk to drive. The place seemed to sparkle from the hilltop.

On the top of the hill here I stand

To witness the sparkling diamonds on the land,

The intoxication of the air numbs my hand

The hills are the gift of God most grand,

To me from higher up the other hill the birds sing a song

For what my heart had been craving for so long,

To protect myself from the cold layers and layers of clothes I wear

The old hills that have stood there naked for a thousand years give me a mocking stare.

They can neither speak nor walk

But secretly and silently to us they talk,

A deep message to all of us they convey

Stand sturdy and strong no matter what comes in your way.

The experience with the car was horrible, but the beauty of the place made us forget it all. We sat on the hilltop for a few minutes and adored the beauty, and then started looking for a hotel. The night had arrived and it had started to snow hard, so we dropped the idea of staying in the tree house that night. Our legs were hurting and we were too scared of taking a taxi again, so we decided to stay in the first hotel we saw. It wasn't very luxurious, but a comfortable place to stay in for the night. We'd just taken a deep breath, drank a few drops of water, tried to recover from the things that had happened, when suddenly another great thing happened. "Fatty, learn some manners. You are not that young that I need to tell you that you shouldn't sit in a way that you move the whole sofa." I teased Samar as I thought he was the reason behind the sudden jerk.

"But I didn't sit that hard. I feel as if along with me everything else is shivering." There was an expression of anxiety on his face like something unusual was happening. "I feel just the same." My voice became low, shocked by the coincidence and also the realization of something bad happening. In no less than two minutes we heard voices yelling, "Run! Earthquake! Go out!" There was a sudden chaos and there was panic all around. Everyone became like a lost ball in high weeds. Maybe the residents of Kashmir knew what an earthquake meant there. It wasn't just an earthquake but a life threat. I believed the same. We weren't completely out of one shock that we came across another. I felt that I was living the last moments of my life and just wanted to bid farewell to my loved ones one last time. But at least I was satisfied with the fact that I was dying with Samar.

We were all like cats on hot bricks except Samar. While we all were rooted to the spot, he was roaming around so calmly, making phone calls, looking here and there. There was not a single sign of fear in him. It was almost as if he felt nothing. He was not even aware of what fear meant. People may call it brave, but for me not feeling fear at all was super scary. But luckily God answered our prayers and there wasn't much damage. At least not to any human being. We breathed a sigh of relief and moved inside the hotel again.

"I am so glad that now I'll have enough tales to narrate to my grandchildren!" Samar laughed.

We were extremely hungry as we hadn't had a single bite since morning. We weren't tensed anymore, but laughing at what all happened with us. Some moments like this leave a permanent mark on our hearts which is completely irremovable. No matter how much more I'll go through, but this particular incident will never be forgotten.

The night was like a beautiful rainbow after a heavy rain. We were eating like those hungry people who hadn't got to eat for ages.

"So, what next for tomorrow?" I asked drinking the hot tomato soup.

"Let's make this trip adventurous!" Samar exclaimed with joy.

"As if it had been any less adventurous!" I grinned.

"We'll go for mountaineering tomorrow."

"Okay, but for now let's go and enjoy the *shikara* ride. Look the night is so beautiful," I said pointing out of the window.

"Okay. When are your parents coming?"

"They'll be here day after tomorrow."

"Great! Really excited to meet them!"

"Me too!" We had a luscious dinner and went for the *shikara* ride. What pleasure it was to watch the starry cold night with the snow-covered trees and small houses can't be described in words. We went to sleep as it had begun to snow hard again and we had had a long tiring day that day.

It was finally the day for mom and dad to arrive and I was very excited and nervous at the same time. Excited because I was going to meet them after a very long time. Nervous because I was dreading that Samar may show them his extra frank nature and say something weird.

"Hello Mom!" I said hugging her again and again and kissing her on the forehead. In these four-five years I hadn't realized how much I had missed her, but when she came in front of my eyes, they couldn't stop sparkling with ecstasy.

"Hello darling! Mamma missed you so much!" Mom said kissing on my cheeks. That's the thing I love the most about my mum, no matter how old I grow, she'll always treat me like a toddler, like her princess whom she loves the most.

"Oh my God Aarika! Do you realise how fat you've become?" Dad can never change. It was his same old way of greeting me and making me laugh.

"Thank you, dad, there wasn't anyone in a while to remind me of that. Now that you've done it, I'll surely shed some weight." I said laughing and hugging dad. The way Samar met mom and dad was shocking. I never expected such courtesy from him. They had a nice long chat for five hours and talked as if they had known each other for years. They seemed to mix up so well.

"Oh God, you two are so adorable," mom said with a bright twinkle in her eyes.

"Mom please shut up. We are just friends," I said scolding her and pinching her hand.

"Mrs. Martins were you aware of your daughter's capabilities to lie so well? Well, for me she's not just my friend. She is like that sunshine whose light has taken away all the darkness from my life, she talks too much but each word she speaks gives immense joy to my tired soul. She's that girl who loves to dance in the rain like a lunatic without caring that people are watching. Her insanity makes it hard to love her, but harder not to love her. She scares the hell out of me some times, but she is the one who has taught me to laugh. She screams like a ghost when she's angry, but that only makes her look cuter. She's scared to do things sometimes, but once she does them, she comes out a winner always. For instance, yesterday, she wasn't agreeing to go for mountaineering but once she did it, she was the first one to reach the top of the mountain. And today I openly confess that I love her. I love her so much! Your parents are here today, you are here; I can't get a better opportunity to ask this. Will you marry me, Aarika?" I didn't understand the need of saying all that, but he came in very good books of my parents.

"Well said son! Very well said!" Dad let his hands in the air and exclaims with joy.

"Oh my God! You know our daughter more than we do! Oh my god, how great it would be to see both my kids getting married before I die! Say yes honey!" Mom looked at me with her twinkling eyes and was extremely delighted.

"Thank you, Samar. I know I am awesome," I just laughed off the whole thing.

"You didn't answer my question, Aarika." He said with a serious look on his face.

Seeing the happiness in mom and dad's eyes, and expectations in Samar's, without even actually wanting to say it, I said, "I need some time." I knew I would never say yes, but for the time being I said that I wanted time. He could never be more than a friend to me. I just didn't see him that way.

***

Kashmir is truly a heaven on earth. Our trip was more amazing than I thought it could ever be. I never thought that mom, dad, and Samar would grow so fond of each other. All our laughs, all our hugs, all the beauty we saw, all the adventures, all the cries when we were saying good bye to each other, everything about that trip is just unforgettable. It was so hard to meet mom and dad after so long and bid farewell in such a short time.

After we got back, we took at least a week's time to narrate all our incidents to Brooke and Flynn. They both were busy so they couldn't join us for the trip. When I told Brooke and Flynn about Samar's proposal, Brooke's excitement knew no bounds. But Flynn wasn't in favour of any hasty steps. But after that trip we all got close to each other. We used to see each other's houses as our second home.

From a rich spoilt brat, Samar became a true gentleman. He even became Kevin's best buddy. With each other's support and innovative ideas, we all reached such heights which we never thought we could climb. But a point came when we were together, but still not completely with each other. Maybe because we gave more priority to our dreams and didn't know how to keep a balance between things. Our life wasn't a beautiful journey anymore but a race to be on the top. I thought then the journey to a destination called love is very tough, yet beautiful. But no matter how beautiful it is, someday, at some point we'll start feeling homesick. Home — the real world — where there's no space for love.

2018
Lost and
Found

Three years had passed and my life was all about go to work, sometimes party, and sleep. But they were the years of great success for me and Kevin. I released many albums, and became a much more renowned singer. Brooke and Flynn started dating. Samar asked me for marriage repeatedly, but I just asked for more time. It had started seeming to both of us that no matter how much time I was given, it would never be enough. But he asked me again today, and I don't know what made me say yes. Mom and dad also thought Samar is the best match for me, maybe because Samar had never shown his true side to them. But I knew what he was. I had seen his dark side.

I did love Samar, but also, I pitied him. I pitied the kind of person he was when we first met. Being with me had transformed him, fortunately in a positive way. That same arrogant person had now begun to go to the orphanage every Sunday with me. He has started helping people and moreover, and is nice to everyone. He has become a human. At least he was trying. Really hard. For once in his life, he is finally happy. He is finally living and enjoying his life. After seeing all this, I just couldn't bring myself to say no when he asked me once again for marriage. Maybe I was tired of waiting for someone to return and give me his approval. Maybe only Samar and I were destined to be together. Maybe nobody could love me like Samar.

"Aarika, are you sure you haven't taken any hurried step? The decision to spend your life with someone is the most important decision. You realise that, don't you?" Flynn was really sceptical about it all. I didn't even know why.

"Shut up Flynn, don't try to influence her. She is a smart, grown up adult who is capable of making her own decisions. I can't even tell you Aarika, how happy I am for you." Brooke hugged me for the hundredth time in the whole day. She was happier than anyone else.

"I don't know if Samar loves you or not, that guy is mystery. We've been friends for five years, yet it feels that I know nothing about him. But you are very simple Aarika. I do know you and

I don't see love in your eyes for him." Flynn again contradicted Brooke. I knew how much Brooke was going to persecute Flynn for this when they were alone.

"How do you even know what love is?" I joined Flynn in his idiocrasy.

"You'll know it when you find it. There are so many feelings imbibed in one simple word. The feeling when you look into their eyes and the whole world fades, nothing else matters. The feeling when you are with them and your heart can't stop yelling, 'Oh God, you are beautiful.' The feeling when you want to hear their voice every waking hour of your day. The feeling when you can't control those haphazard sensations flowing within you. The feeling when you find peace in their arms that no song, no hill or no sea could give you. The feeling when you can't stop smiling each time anyone talks about them. The way I can't stop feeling around Brooke. That is love, my girl. And you don't deserve to settle for anything less than love, Aarika. Don't settle for anything that isn't love!" I had never seen Flynn so serious and emotional in these three years. I didn't know why he was so dissatisfied by my decision.

"Tell me honestly Brooke, how many romantic movies have you made him watch recently? The effect is too prominent. Flynn dear, not everyone is lucky enough to get your kind of love. But I do love your best friend in my own kind of way. Don't you ever doubt that! Your friend is in very safe and lovable hands." The argument went on for another hour until Brooke left the room.

I agreed with Flynn to think about it once, but in my heart, I was quite sure and happy about my decision. The love that Flynn described was not meant for this ugly corrupted world, it was just meant for the beautiful, ethereal world of books and movies.

***

It had been two weeks since Samar and I had been engaged. I had come to New York for a concert and the sky was clear, clear light blue painted through the horizon, the kind of beautiful in which you'd like yourself to drown in.

The air filled with love, carried messages of the distant lovers. I mean the flowers and sky by that. Everything around was so admirable so I decided to go for a walk and look after the preparations of the concert myself. At 6 in the evening I had walked out as a girl in high spirits, and by 6:30 p.m. I was even more joyful when I saw the happy, excited faces assembling in the ground. As there was still time for the concert to start, the number of the people wasn't much, so I could see the people present there clearly.

By 6:45 p.m. I felt my heart fall into the pit of my stomach. My joy turned to horror. My excitement turned into pain and anger. My whole world stopped. I was having sudden attacks of dizziness. But I just couldn't stop this time. I had to go. I had to run. Really fast. Before he was gone again. I had to stop him. I ran after him and held his hands so tightly that there was no scope left for him to run again.

"Why did you do this to me?" My eyes were burning with anger but his eyes were smiling as usual. He didn't utter a single word and kept looking at me, not moving his eyes away from mine as if he wasn't guilty of anything. As if he hadn't done anything wrong. His chuck hazel eyes were shining at me. When he didn't reply. I held his hand tightly and took him backstage. He was back. Ayan was back. Shanaya aunty too came running after us.

"Why the hell did you do it! How could you just leave me alone like that, without even bidding a good bye?" I yelped on the top of my voice and held his arms tightly almost hurting them and then finally gave him a tight slap when he still wasn't saying anything. "Where were you? Where the heck were you all this while? Where were you when I needed you the most?" Both Shanaya aunty and he stood motionless and still. "Speak up Ayan! Speak up!" Each part of mine wanted to hurt him. Tear his every tissue apart. After ten long years how could he return just like that! You see the passion of this friendship? People don't take more than a day to even forget their close ones. But here it had been more than ten years and each memory was still afresh, fresher than it should have been.

"I am proud of you my friend!" He said hugging me with tears in his eyes.

"Don't you dare! You've lost all your rights to hug me! Now answer me!" I said pushing him away. He stood there biting his lips as if that would help him to control his tears. His hazel eyes that used to smile from his cheeks were now shedding tears. "Aarika look I've got explanation for all this. But I am sorry, I should have told you."

"Told me what?"

"I just came out of the nasty jaws of death Aarika. Do you remember the day when we went to that forest? How I had started to feel seedy? That was when I knew that symptoms of my disease had started showing up. Thinking that I only had a few days to live, I felt very depressed and thus did the things I did. The nerve cells in my brain had started to breakdown. My behaviour, me hurting you and everyone, were all the result of my disease."

"What disease?!" I became even more panicky and my anger turned to shock now.

"Huntington's Chorea. I inherited it from dad. All the psychiatric symptoms in me were due to this only. I wasn't even able to walk on my own. I had lost weight to an extent you can't even imagine. Or for that matter I didn't even realize what all I was doing to you. I would wake up in the middle of the night and stand before mom with a knife in my hand. It usually kills people like it killed dad, but luckily when I came to America, doctors had invented a new drug for the cure of Huntington's chorea. The trials of that drug were going on and fortunately it happened to work for me."

"Oh God! Who could think that a person who was larger than life was going through something like this? I misunderstood you so much and I am so sorry for that!" I hadn't felt any guiltier than this in my whole life. But also, I was so, so thankful to God for saving Ayan's life. I hugged him so tightly, never wanting him to leave ever again. I felt the peace I shouldn't be feeling. It was a dreamlike peace.

"Had I been not so amazing, you wouldn't have become such a great singer today. Now go, your fans are waiting for you," He said laughing and wiping his tears, trying to make the atmosphere lighter.

"No, I am not going anywhere. I want to spend this time with you."

"Honey go, you both have plenty of time now and I am eager to hear you sing." I had to go when Shanaya aunty insisted. With him all my happiness had returned. I couldn't have asked for more. I was like a dog with two tails that day. That day I didn't have to fake a smile, but a big natural grin was there on my face. I was sure it was going to be one of my best performances ever.

"Where's Shanaya aunty?" I directly rushed to Ayan after the concert ended, but couldn't see Shanaya aunty anywhere.

"She's on a call. Martins, you still didn't sing nicely. But don't worry now that I am here you will one day." He pulled my hair. If your best friend ever compliments you then you should think they are suffering from some mental illness. But they are the ones who encourage you when you need encouragement the most. No matter what happened in Ayan's life, he was still the same idiotic, jovial person, bringing smiles on others' faces. He wanted to cherish each and every moment of his life, not let any moment be lifeless.

"You still do that." I grinned. When we were kids, he used to pull my hair all the time. It was so good to have someone do this after so long.

"Aarika, where were you? I had been looking for you everywhere. By the way you rocked it today!" Samar came running towards us. My eyes were already looking at him with guilt because I knew that now I would spend most of my time with Ayan.

"Uh, meet Ayan. Remember the guy I told you about?" I said with a little hesitation.

"Oh yes, I do. How can I forget such a special friend of yours?" Samar said hugging Ayan. That hug wasn't a friendly one, but more of a kind to check the power of the other person. Ayan too hugged Samar back and started shaking hands with him. They shook hands for about fifteen minutes staring directly into each other's eyes, giving each other absurd looks, without uttering a single word and I stood there thinking about occurrence of the whole episode. The brightness of both their faces had faded away.

"Ayan this is Samar, my friend."

"Sorry but I think Aarika forgot to mention that I am her fiancé," Samar said proudly.

"Oh good. Congratulations, Aarika!" I knew that sarcastic tone of Ayan. It was like Samar was that extra bright light that Ayan couldn't bear to see. Ayan didn't even want to show that much courtesy to face towards Samar while talking to him. So, he turned to the other side.

"By the way Aarika, how did he get here? Hadn't he become mad? Who left his cage open? What if he hurts someone?"

"Excuse me?" Ayan turned and retorted.

"No, no, nothing! He has this habit of joking all the time. Don't take him seriously." For the first time I had to lie to my own best friend. I clearly knew that Samar wasn't joking.

"To be honest, I wasn't joking this time," Samar bended down and whispered in my ear.

"Samar, can you please cut it out?"

Seeing both of them standing face to face I was stunned that how could two strangers hate each other so much. Just at the right time Samar's phone rang and he went to some other place to talk. Had he stood there for another minute, a war would have begun. I wondered if they'd just met then what made their eyes burn with anger. I was curious to know why they were so cheesed off with each other.

"Seriously Aarika, you got no other person to marry? Out of millions of people you had to choose this snobby idiotic person?" Ayan said in disgust.

"Aarika, I have to run back to London. I've got a very urgent meeting. See you there. Come back safely. Take care."

"She's a five-year-old right, that the kidnappers will abduct her?" Ayan said sarcastically.

"It's better if people with a class like you don't interfere in matters of people of high society." Samar said with his same devilish grin.

"Aarika tell him to leave or else he will not go back in a good condition," Ayan yelled on the top of his voice.

"Oh, you will beat me, you dumbass?"

"Samar, you must be getting late. See you in London. Bye," I kissed him on the cheek, trying to lessen the heat.

"Take care. Bye." Samar hugged me and went.

"Thank God, he's gone. Gosh how can you even tolerate a guy like that?"

"Leave him. I have loads of things to ask and tell you. But you and Shanaya aunty are going with me to the hotel."

"I'll come along but not sure about mom. When are you going back?"

"Monday and you are coming with me to London."

“That’s like two days away! How can I come all of a sudden? I am a busy owner of a hotel now,” Ayan said laughing.

“Oh boy, finally your dream of running a hotel came true! I can’t even express my happiness for you!” I hugged him tightly.

“By the way, can’t you just come for a few days to London?”

“The good news is, I can. Mom and my dear friend Brandon handle my work brilliantly. He is doing his internship anyway. But first let’s go home and take some clothes and other things.” Ayan came and we went back to the hotel. I was so excited for the night was going to be a night of great fun, in which I could be myself — no makeup, no heavy clothes — just me.

***

“Why didn’t you ever try to contact me Ayan?” I asked as we sat on the bed comfortably in our pyjamas with ice cream cups in our hands.

“I tried. I wanted to talk to you so badly. The night before Kevin left, he came to my place and asked me to stay away from you. And then the next day I got a call from Priyanka aunty and she told me if I really considered you a friend and loved you, then I should never meet you again. That’s why I avoided you in school or anywhere else. I had realized that I was the biggest threat to your life. Then, my condition became so bad that I wasn’t in my senses and soon after I left for America.

All that my life revolved around for six long years was doctors, appointments and meds and therapies. No one will ever know how hard it was to not lose hope. I was confined to four walls of my room. Who knows better than you that there’s no worse torture for me than to sit in one place all day long. But then I was surprised to know that the treatment worked for me. You were the first one whom I wanted to inform that I could live. But it was hard for me to even think of the fact that you’d want me back in your life after all I had done. You were all over the news. God, you were everywhere. I saw that you were happy and

I didn't want to interrupt. And then I convinced myself that I was too late and I could never have you back in my life. I thought I had lost you forever. But luckily you saw me today."

"How could you even think that? You don't know how badly I needed you at every point of my life. Each moment I would tell myself I hated you, tried my best to forget you but in these ten years I don't think there has been a single day when I didn't think about you."

"Maybe it's rightly said that everything has its own time. That wasn't the time when you, I and Kevin were meant to be together. Maybe now it is. But you can't even imagine what I went through." He told me all about Huntington's chorea. God, it still gives me goosebumps. You don't even realise and slowly everything deteriorates and then all of a sudden, you are dead. He became so weak that he always needed someone to move him. He would go to places without even realizing where he was going. It hurts so much when you don't know what's happening around you, you don't know what you are doing or for that matter you can't even hold a small pin in your hand. You become so hideous that you are scared of looking at yourself. You are physically alive but you die inside. But he was fortunate enough to survive all of that.

"Let's not recall the past now, but treasure the moment we are in right now. By the way, look at you! All transformed into a new person, huh? But don't you expect me to compliment you for that. You'll always be the same chimpanzee for me." Ayan changed the topic when he felt that all of it was becoming very plaintive. No matter if I met Ayan after ten years or hundred years, he would never miss a chance to make fun of me.

"I can see you are also doing a lot of body building, but don't worry that wouldn't make any difference to your donkey like appearance," I told him.

"Look, I don't want to ruin the moment, but tell me how are we gonna meet after this month? You can't leave Shanaya aunty alone with all the work for more than a month." In this excitement I forgot that Ayan and I now lived in far off lands and it would be very difficult for us to meet.

"Okay so here's the good news. Mom signed a contract with dad's friend Joe who lives in Stratford, so we are planning on shifting there, and if one's very keen to meet someone then it's very close to London. My cousin will be handling the hotel in New York, and mom and I will take charge of the hotel in Stratford. My uncle and I are partners. So, he'll be taking charge of the hotel in New York. I wouldn't have been able to do this without him. Now that we are going to London, I'll meet Joe and finalise everything."

"Oh my God! Oh my God! I can't believe it! And also, this is random, but you know what Kevin is getting married!" I said dancing and jumping in the room.

"What! What! What! Oh my God! It's unbelievable! Time to celebrate!" He too joined me and opened a bottle of drink.

"By the way, may I ask you why you and Samar behaved that way? Do you guys know each other?"

"I met him for the first time today. Who would like to keep an acquaintance with a person like him? He started it first. And if you know me well, you would know how hard I controlled myself to not humiliate him. Otherwise one sentence was enough for his ego to shatter."

People say that girls are very complicated, like extremely hard to understand. But after seeing Ayan and Samar, my thinking has changed.

***

"By the way, you know what? You should write your vows on a toilet paper." Ayan was all drunk. He looked at his glass with droopy eyes. Even though he was barely able to open his eyes, I could see a sadness in his eyes which knew no bounds.

"Ayan, just give me that glass, you are out of your mind. God, you are so drunk."

"Oh, I haven't touched this thing in years. Let me compensate that today. And—and you know why you should write your vows on a toilet paper? Because your man, Sa—mar is a piece of shit." He said giggling and scratching his head unconsciously.

"And what are you if Samar is a piece of shit? The remaining shit? Now leave that bloody glass! Okay enough now! I cannot keep my eyes open for a minute more now. I am going to bed. We just have three hours and then I have an important meeting. You too go to your room now. Good night." I turned off the lights and fell on my bed comfortably. After ten minutes, just when I was about to fell asleep, Ayan shouted in my ear "Martins, are you asleep yet?" He turned off the AC, shut the door, and ran away. He could never change. He used to do that even when we were kids. He clearly knew that I was asleep, still he would come intentionally to me, shout in my ear and wake me up.

The night went just with a blink of an eye, talking, singing, and dancing with each other. It was as if through all of those years I was physically living, but emotionally dead. But that day everything came to life. I always used to wonder when Ayan and I were kids, if our friendship would remain as it was back then, if fate separated Ayan and me. That was bound to happen, even though our dreams were similar, they were not same. But that day, I was free of all the doubts. When I woke up the next day, I wished that I could live those moments over and over again. But someone rightly said, "The mistake is thinking that there can be an antidote to uncertainty."

2018
Wedding bells,
Wedding bells
all the awy

So, another chapter of my life started here. Kevin's wedding. Three days after, Ayan and I went back to London. I was excited to see Kevin's expression as he still didn't know anything that happened.

"You hide behind me and then scare Kevin the same way you scared me when we were kids." I said to Ayan, handing him the ghost mask that I brought from New York.

"God, look at us who can say that we are grown up, responsible adults," he said laughing and wearing the mask.

"You maybe, I still love that child in me and I won't ever let it go," I giggled.

"It's good to see Martins speaking such cool things. I mean I feel so good that I have influenced someone to this extent that I have transformed her completely."

"Shut up and be ready. I am ringing the bell now," I scolded him jokingly.

"Hello my sissy, how are ... who's this standing behind you?" A ghastly whiteness spread over his face.

"Who's there? I don't see anyone," I acted as if I knew nothing.

"You move away. Don't you forget I am your elder brother and you can't trick me into something like this!" He moved forward and quickly removed the mask from Ayan's face.

"Ayan! Aarika, why is he here?" Kevin's tone lowered and his grin faded.

"Don't lash out Kevin! I'll tell you everything," I said trying to pacify him.

***

"Ahaa! My long-lost bro is back!" Kevin neither said sorry, nor tried to create any atmosphere of despondency, but just hugged Ayan tightly after I told him everything.

"Big people huh? Getting married? How could you not care to invite me? Who would make everyone laugh then?" Ayan started punching Kevin with a smirk on his face.

"Gosh she told you as well! Since the past six months she's been blabbering about my wedding to each and every person she is meeting! By the way you don't need any invitation. You are the host now!"

"Don't just talk about me, look at yourself. No groom would've been as excited as you are," I said interrupting.

"Stop it you both! You know how difficult it is? How tensed I am? I am sure Rihanna will run away the next day of our wedding."

"And why is it so?" Ayan and I said in unison.

"Boy! How can one tolerate me?" Kevin cried dramatically.

"Oh, I agree. That's one of the most difficult tasks that can be assigned to someone." I giggled.

"When she has been tolerating you since a year, she can love you for her entire life. Love makes people do wonderful things! But still I would like to do some inspection. Call her over for dinner tonight," Ayan spoke in a fake voice, trying to sound like a wise old man.

There is a different excitement about the wedding atmosphere. Even the same mundane house started feeling so full of life. I hadn't felt more responsible in my life than I felt when mom gave me all the responsibilities for Kevin's wedding. She always loved the clothes here in London, so I had to do the shopping for everyone. No matter how renowned personality I was, I was foremost my parents' daughter, and my brother's sister. Therefore, I was given the complete responsibility without any hesitation. In this hustle bustle, I almost forget about Samar. When I checked my phone, I saw his messages.

Samar read all the messages but didn't reply to a single one. I didn't give much thought to it as only a month was left for Kevin's wedding and when Ayan was there how could I do anything else. I earlier thought that Ayan, Samar and I would make a really great group, but when I recalled what happened at the concert, I realized that it is utter foolishness and it would only lead to awkward situations for me.

We didn't do much today as all three of us were very tired. We just enjoyed each other's company, which was the most pleasant thing for us to do.

***

By the night time we had regained our energy and eagerly waited for Rihanna. Though I had known her for three or four months, I never actually got a chance to know her, so I was really excited to spend the night with her. Ayan wore a black hoodie with beige pants and sneakers. I wore a maroon peplum dress, and Kevin didn't care about anything or anyone, so he wore his most comfortable and favourite printed pink pyjama with a grey t-shirt.

"Hey Ayan, am I not looking way too great tonight?" I said proudly flipping my hair.

"Hahaha the chimpanzee just called, and he asks you to give his face back," he said chuckling. I could even hear Kevin break into a loud laughter in the other room.

Rihanna finally joined us. She was so pretty that she looked no less than a princess in her bottle green silk frock paired with high heels and a pearl necklace.

"So Rihanna, would you like to share the story with us of how you first met Kevin?" Ayan sat in front of Rihanna at the dining table like a cop investigating her.

"That's a bit embarrassing Kevin, if you don't mind can I tell him?" Ah that cute, innocent lady! That expression of innocence and sweetness on her face! She looked so adorable!

"Ah, he's my bro, why would I feel embarrassed in front of him? Also, he's your investigator for now and nothing should be hidden from the police so go ahead," Kevin laughed.

"Okay. So, a year back in December, on a Sunday, it was one of the coldest days in the history of London, and it was snowing really hard. It was twelve in the night and my doorbell rang. And there he was, standing, drenched from head to toe.

"Madam, if you don't mind may I use the toilet? All your neighbours happen to be sleeping." He was completely red, quivering and barely able to speak. After using the toilet, he wanted to leave, but was in desperate need of help. His car had stopped working. I was generous enough to let him stay and I made coffee for both of us. In no less than ten minutes his jokes started and after a few hours there we were, laughing like lunatics, like we were long lost best friends or something. I never knew I could connect so well with someone in such a short span of time. After that we started meeting often and my life completely changed. He filled all the empty spaces in my life," she replied and Kevin was all red like a tomato.

"But what exactly made you fall for him?" Ayan interrogated further.

"His lunacies, his flying freely like a bird all the time. I mean just look at him right now. We all here so concerned about our looks, but there he is only concerned about his comfort. Everything is just so different about him! He has changed my perspective towards life and made me feel loved."

"Wow Rihanna! I am impressed!" Ayan's investigation finally came to an end and Kevin's eyes were filled with joy, a joy I had never seen before.

"Three cheers for the lovely couple! Hip-hip Hurrah! Hip-hip Hurrah! Hip-hip Hurrah!" Ayan, I and all the servants cheered for them. We had dinner and after chatting for a while Kevin dropped Rihanna back. We had been lazing around since morning so all three of us were still full of energy, so we turned the music on, wore our pyjamas and dancing shoes, and danced the whole night to celebrate the joy of Kevin's wedding. It was like I was footloose and fancy-free.

"Man, you've found just the perfect girl! I mean if she can love you for something as poor as your sense of humour, then leave the worries of her leaving you ever," Ayan laughed.

"You, don't you forget where you got that attitude from. And don't mess with your daddy," Kevin said lifting the collar of his t-shirt.

"Jokes apart, for the first time in my life Kevin, I actually want to say that I am proud of you!" I said merrily. I was the one happiest of all because I got along really well with Rihanna. She has such a pure soul that the moment you stand next to her, you start getting positive vibes.

***

I didn't even know how almost a month passed by. Each one of these days was a joyride. Not even one day I felt as if I had been separated from Ayan for ten long years. All this while he had felt so close to my heart even when he was miles away. Ayan finalized the deal with Joe. He went back to New York for a while but he's here again for Kevin's wedding. He and Shanaya aunty would be shifting next year in May. That's a very long time, but also this year is almost over. But Brooke had been driving me crazy. She kept disapproving of Ayan living at my place. She thought we had fallen in love or something and then kept showing me the ring on my finger, kept reminding me that I was Samar's now. I was his asset now and no one else could put his eyes on me. She was weirdly rude to Ayan. Whenever Ayan called her Brooke, she said "You have no right to call me by that name. I am just Brooklyn for you." Silly bitch, she doesn't understand that this is not the love between lovers, but between long lost best friends. Falling in love with Ayan would be the last possible thing for me. When he returned from New York, I took him for city tour. He had been really busy with his hotel stuff so we hadn't got time for that until now. We first went to the church and prayed.

If Ayan and I were together, then that meant that the most important part of our day is food. So, we had breakfast more than ten people in London could have had, and we were so full that we were not even able to move. I realized then what a big foodie I am! We rested there for a few minutes and then went on for the Hop-on Hop-off bus tour in which we saw the Tower of London, Buckingham Palace, Westminster Abbey, St. Paul's Cathedral, and Trafalgar square. I had been to all these places before, but with Ayan the excitement was different. Those same old places started seeming new to me and I looked at them differently. After that we went to Warner Bros. Studio — The making of Harry Potter, which was behind the scenes tour. We saw all the props and costumes used in the movies and glimpses of scenes from it. It was the best of all and a great pleasure for Harry Potter fans like me and Ayan.

Our next destination was London Dungeon, which is an extraordinarily exciting place that took us back to the London's past's most horrible bits, and we were altogether drawn into another world, where the boundaries between reality and the past blurred. Our final destination was Madame Tussauds where we got our pictures clicked with the wax statues of William Shakespeare, Her Majesty, Adele, Daniel Radcliffe, Amitabh Bachhan, and many others. I dreamt that my statue may also be there someday. After coming out from the restaurant where we had dinner, we saw a huge crowd standing on the other corner of the street and heard the sound of drums, violins, and other instruments playing there with people dancing. It all sent vibrations through my body.

"I dare you to go and dance there," Ayan challenged me, hanging his jacket on his back. For the first time I saw his chuck hazel eyes looking at me in a way as if they thought that I couldn't do the task they challenged me to.

"Do you really think that would be difficult for me? But I'll do it only on one condition," I said removing my jacket and flipping my hair.

"What?"

"You'll have to join me sometime later."

"Okay done. Now go!"

When I went there, I saw those people dancing so flawlessly, but then I remembered that I was a great dancer in my time too. I signalled them to move back and started dancing to the beat of the drum.

"Whoa! Whoa! Whoa! Girl you got some moves!" Ayan cheered from the crowd and everyone started clapping. I started with some gorgeous and really perfect moves, but then I thought that was what everyone was doing there, so I ended up dancing and jumping. Sometime later Ayan joined me too, and I was damn sure people there would have never ever seen two people dance with more insanity than we did. I never ever thought that doing something like that could be so much fun. All I cared about was my image in the past two or three years, but now I realized that I had been missing out the real fun. What a pleasure it was to dance like insane people in the snow!

"Oh my God it was so amazing!" Before people started throwing stones on us or I lost my reputation, we ran away from there, guffawing like lunatics.

"I know right?" Ayan said removing snow from his jacket.

"Right." I was laughing so hard that my eyes were almost shut. Maybe that's why I didn't even notice that car coming at such a high speed.

"Aarika! Be careful! Are you mad! Oh god, something really bad has just been prevented! I am going to hold your hand like two-year old kids now and carry you around these streets." I looked at our entwined fingers. I didn't know why that just made me so joyous and nervous at the same time.

We then went to the ice cream parlour and I brought Death by Chocolate, and Ayan went for Vanilla with Choco Chip.

"Martins, you know what? You are one of the very few things that I am grateful for in my life." he said as he took a bite of his ice cream and laughed a little.

"Ayan, did you meet anyone this while, I mean do you have a girlfriend?" I didn't know why this thought struck me all of a sudden.

"No um... I mean yes. We hang out together, have fun, we make fun of each other, but if we don't see each other our day is incomplete. God, she moves me, she makes me crazy." As he spoke each word, I could feel my heart sinking. I should be happy for him, I should have teased him. Why did I feel as if suddenly streams of pain were flowing inside me?

"Oh really? If she's so dear to you, why am I getting to know about her now?" All of a sudden, without any reason I had become so rude to him.

"I don't know, there were just so many other things to tell you."

"Oh," I said with great suspicion. "What's her name and how did you meet her?"

"Cathy. She's the receptionist in my hotel."

"Good."

"Hey Aarika, can you click my picture with these lights? Cathy wants to see my pictures. Just got her text. Make sure that I look hot." He handed me his phone and started posing.

"Sure." It made me so furious. Ayan hated it if someone clicked his pictures. But was he so much in love that he had succumbed to getting his photos clicked? I threw his phone, almost breaking it.

"Damn girl! Calm down. What has happened to you?" Ayan was just as shocked as I was.

“Tell Cathy that her death is coming if she doesn’t leave you.” I couldn’t help but cry and shouted at him.

“Martins, sit down. I was just kidding. She is hypothetical. My receptionist is a guy, Aaron.”

“Oh well. Good for her. If she had existed, I would chop her into pieces.” I didn’t know what had gotten inside me. But I got a weird sense of relief knowing that Ayan was just joking about Cathy.

“God, why would you want to kill my girlfriend?” It was all a joke to him and he was laughing madly.

“Because idiot, I love you! You moron!”

“What?” I could see beads of sweat on his face.

I looked right into his chuck hazel eyes and said, “I know Samar is my fiancé, I know we are meeting after so long, I know that all this is going to be a mess, but today I want to confess something. If I ever loved anyone, then it’s you, if I want to spend my life with someone, then it’s you. If I feel that anyone who loves me for my insanity then it’s you, and only you! And right now, I myself have no idea what all I am saying.”

He raised his eyebrow and looks at me with great suspicion. And then finally after a long silence he said, “Absolutely a very poor prank Aarika.” Had I been in his place I would have felt exactly the same. He is my best friend since we were kids. We know each other’s insecurities, our dark secrets. We make fun of each other in the worst possible ways. How can I fall in love with him? But the truth is I am in love with him. Even I wasn’t aware of this fact until then.

“I am serious, Ayan. I am in love with you.” Still looking right into his eyes, I replied with a very serious expression on my face.

“Oh. My. God.” He moved back with hands on his mouth and the ice cream dropped from his hand. He was flabbergasted.

“Yes, Ayan I love you. I love you with all my heart!” I yelled loudly sitting amidst the snow and the well-lighted up trees.

“Aarika, I am afraid I can’t say the same for you. I mean, I never thought about us in that way. And you shouldn’t either.” Ayan tried to be serious but I could almost see his smile. It just broke my heart. At this very moment I realised how much I had loved him always and now I couldn’t imagine myself being with anyone else. I couldn’t help but cry like a small kid.

When I didn’t stop crying for another half an hour, Ayan came to me laughing so hard that he couldn’t even breathe.

“Oh God Aarika. I was only kidding I know you are going to make fun of me forever for this and this is so not like my thing, but the truth is that I have been in love with you since we were seventeen! Oh no!” he said giggling. He was so happy that I could see tears of happiness in his eyes.

“Sorry, what?” I was even more shocked than Ayan was a few seconds back.

“Your shock shocks me. I always tried to make you feel special. I thought you always knew,” he said lifting his hands in air.

“How was I supposed to know? You were so nice to everyone. All the time! You made everyone feel special. It was like just like your eyes, your ears, your nose; being nice was also a part of you!”

“Oh Aarika, you’ve always been such an idiot. You probably don’t remember but that day in the rainbow park I wanted to tell you this only. But you fell asleep, and then I couldn’t gather my nerves to tell you because I didn’t want to break your heart. I knew the symptoms of my disease had started to show up and I would have to leave you anyway. Oh my God, I am going crazy! Where are the rings?” he asked giggling. I threw the ice-cream in my hand and rolled the tissue and made two rings out of it. I put one on his finger and gave him the other to put on mine.

"Maybe this insanity is what makes me love you so much," he whispered in my ear, kissed me on my forehead, and sat beside me.

We watched the stars and fought with each other about how for so long we had hidden our feelings from each other. The beauty of the whole moment vanished when a thought struck Ayan. "What about Samar, Aarika?"

"He'll understand." I knew he won't, I knew we were in a big mess, but just to pacify Ayan, I said so.

"What if he doesn't?"

"Let's not think about that right now," I said and hugged him tightly as we enjoyed the stelliferous night.

I have no idea how I am even going to tell him this, let alone making him understand.

Under the stars I stood, painting his every bit on the canvas of my heart. I found the scenes of those romantic movies to be so useless, but now I could relate to everything. Everything in those movies was making sense to me. I saw all my comfort in his loving arms, and in him my whole universe. I was shocked to see this sudden realisation, but at the same time happy as well. I felt as if there was music in the air, and Ayan and I were the only creatures alive.

"Tomorrow the first thing we'll do is go to his house. I don't want his expectations to last any longer than they should. They are only going to hurt him. And I don't want that." Ayan said sternly. I just couldn't stop looking at him without tears in my eye. I was so, so proud of my choice. I couldn't thank God enough for making me realise before it was too late.

***

"Samar, I don't know how to go about this. I am ss..sorry, I can't marry you," I said keeping the ring in his hands.

"But why? Is it because of the douche, that stupid asshole standing behind you? Did he say something?" Samar was still polite, but I knew what he was going through. His fists were clenched tightly, and his nails were almost hurting his hands.

"Yes, it is because of this douche. I am in love with this stupid asshole. And I can't help it!" I said trying to control tears of my guilt.

"It's okay. I just wanted you to be happy darling, remember? But dare you show your hellish face in my bloody house ever again. If you do, I am not sure if you'll go back alive. Kick your stupid asses out of my house now. Just leave." Samar had never behaved like this. I had seen his worst side. But never like this. He pushed me so hard that I almost fell down and he shut the door without saying anything more.

I didn't blame Samar for behaving the way he did. I couldn't understand his pain, but I knew he was going through a lot. I would have sacrificed my feelings if I could, but now things were pretty much out of my hands, for I was completely drowned in Ayan's love. And I realised, that by marrying Samar I would have robbed myself of one of the best feelings in the world. Love. Love is being there for each other. Love is caring and spending time with each other. But love is not just limited to this. The theory of love is much wider and complex. Love is friendship, love is laughing until your stomach hurts, love is understanding each other better than anyone else can. Love is being a part of each other's craziness.

I had never felt any crazier than this in my whole life. I was not tired of staring at the same face for hours. Sometimes it felt as if it all was senseless, and the other times nothing else seemed to make any sense at all.. I couldn't believe I was so beautifully, so deeply, so madly in love, the thing that I had stopped believing in years ago. This feeling was so new. I felt like going to each and every corner of the world and shout and tell everyone that 'Yes! I am in love.'

Me and Ayan had been making Kevin crazy for he was the only one we could share our feelings with. Kevin told me that Ayan had been acting even weirder than me. But Ayan had actually been acting weirdly for the past two-three days. He just didn't let me come inside his room. And neither he came out. I wondered what he had been doing lately. Brooke hadn't spoken to me for weeks. She was insanely mad at me for doing what I did. I knew she'd be fine in a week or two. I really hoped she was fine in a week or two.

***

I was blindfolded and Ayan drove me somewhere. I was shocked to see that Ayan knew any place here in London. I was pushed inside a room and the cloth on my eyes was removed. It was a dark room. I suspected Ayan of planning some weird pranks.

"Ayan! What are you up to? And, where are you?" I started panicking as I was really scared of dark rooms since that incident happened to me in high school.

"Just wait and watch Martins!" He yelled from outside. All of a sudden soft music started playing and dim lights were switched on. The song, I realised later, was the first song sung by me. The light first fell on a painting. I couldn't believe that a painting could be so real. It was my painting. My eyes, my ears, the tiny mole on my nose—just the same. There were many paintings. I couldn't decide which one was the best. Each one had its own beauty. Each one was perfect in its own way. But the last one just made me cry. Half of Ayan's face and half of my face was painted. It was just so spectacular. I wondered who made all those paintings, but they were the most beautiful ones I had ever seen.

"So, how did you like the surprise?" Ayan came inside the room and asked me as proudly as he could.

“I hadn’t even thought in the wildest dreams that you could do something like this. When you locked me inside this dark room, all I expected of you was to play some weird pranks. But this? God, I am impressed.” I replied, not even expressing half of my actual happiness. I liked picking on Ayan so much, that expression on his face then was just adorable and priceless.

“Days of effort and this is what I get. Wow, I am a proud boyfriend.” He said walking out of the room, trying to act angry. He looked super cute right now.

“Ayan! Wait. I was just teasing you. I loved it a lot. And I loved it more because it was something beyond my expectations. I never expected something like this from a person like you. I never knew that you had even a modicum of romance inside you. God, what else have I failed to figure out about you?” I said hugging him tightly and messing his hair. “And these paintings, I don’t have any words for them. Who made them?”

“The artist of these paintings is popularly known as Monsieur Ayan.”

“What! I can believe anything but not this!”

“Your believing or not believing won’t change the fact.” He seemed angry now.

“It’s good. At least my company made you of some use.” I teased him more.

“Go on with the crap. I am listening,” he gave a sarcastic smile.

“Brooklyn, Lester, thanks for your help, you can come in now.” He stepped half out of the door to call in Brooke and Flynn.

“What is going on here! Brooke? Flynn you too were a part of this? You guys are unbelievable.” I said, my mouth still wide open. How could Ayan make that stubborn Brooke show up after weeks! I thought she was going to need a thousand more apologies.

"How else do you think this moron mastered painting within few days? Ayan what are you waiting for? Do it!" Brooke scolded him.

"I know Martins, it's hard for you to believe that I have fallen so crazily in love with you because all I've ever done is scorn and taunt you. All I've ever done is dump my girlfriends within a week. But this time without any doubts, I can claim that this is forever. Years ago, when I bought my first guitar, I thought that was the maximum love I could have for something. Five years later when I met you, I thought I couldn't be capable of loving any more than this. But my love has grown more and more for you with every passing second. When I saw you dancing to the beats of the morning sun today, I thought I loved you more than any man could ever love a woman. But just now I understood that my previous love was just a grain of sand against my love right now, in this moment which is a universe of beaches. You make me fall in love with you over and over again. I know I never believed in marriage and stuff, but see what you've made of me. Ah the jeans are too tight but I am gonna bend anyway. Will you marry me, Aarika Crazy Martins?"

This was ethereal. That ring was dreamlike! Something like this didn't exist. How could such a beautiful moment exist!

"Yes, a hundred billion thousand million times YES! I will marry you Ayan Insane Oberoi!" I did not need more than a second to reply this time for every part of me knew vividly how madly I was in love with him. I went and hugged him tightly, kissing him side by side. Every atom of his flesh felt as precious as my own. I felt every feeling of Flynn's description of love. That peace, that fading of the world, everything. He was right, I knew love when I saw it.

"You are going to have a hard time telling me how many zeroes there are in a hundred billion thousand million." He laughed and then kissed me again. I could see Brooke and Flynn shedding a tear or two. It was an equally happy moment for them.

Also, something that made me the happiest was the fact that Brooke had accepted Ayan, my love.

"Won't you tell her Ayan, who chose the ring?" Brooke smirked and punched Ayan on the shoulder.

"Had it not been for Brooklyn, you'd still be wearing a tissue on your finger. So many shops, so many designs just drove me mad. How do you girls even manage to shop!"

"So damn right bro! Brooke takes just an hour to buy the whole shop. I won't be able to do that even in four days." Here we have the boys, unaware of a woman's capabilities.

"Flynn Lester, you've got a superwoman in the form of your girlfriend. Ayan you can call me Brooke. It would save you some time." Brooke laughed again, she was happier than any of us.

"Ayan, now that all of us are engaged, what say for a combined wedding? Double wedding, double fun!" said Flynn in an excited tone.

"No! Never!" Brooke and I yelled in unison and then started laughing. No girl would ever agree to that. No girl wants divided attention on her wedding.

"Brooke, I can't tell you how happy I am that you accepted Ayan. I hope you understand it wasn't my fault. You know what love is!" Brooke and I had a night stay after weeks, I was really cherishing that time.

"It's hard not to accept that jackass. He's crazy, but maybe the best guy in this world. If I hadn't loved Flynn so much, I would have probably fallen for him." It made me a bit angry, but I knew she was joking as she was all red from all the laughing.

"Better mind your words girl!"

"By the way, you didn't know about any of our meetings? Flynn, he and I met a lot of times. He had to toil hard for convincing me, but Flynn knew he was the one for you when we first met." Ayan did know how to impress everyone. He knew if I hadn't got Brooke's approval I wouldn't have been as happier as I am now with this relationship.

"We both finally found the bearers of our craziness. I am so, so, grateful, I may even cry. Can you believe how much we are going to shop once we are done with Kevin's wedding!" Three weddings in the way. That's too much happiness to handle!

"Aarika, did you check on Samar? How is he handling all this? He is neither picking my calls, nor Flynn's." Brooke's face saddened all of a sudden.

"He said he'd kill me if I ever show up again. I did try to call him and reach him on social media. But he's ignoring me without any shame."

"He is not doing anything shameful, it's natural and expected. I think you should talk to him once again and end it all on good terms. If not anything else, we all can hang out again as friends. I really miss those days, that endless laughter." I agreed with Brooke, though I knew it couldn't end on good terms now.

***

I went to Samar's place the next morning but I saw Alyssa, his assistant, and him walking in his garden. I didn't why he was with her. He always said that she was irritating, but they both were looking really happy. I won't judge him because I know you can find love in the most unexpected people. I was really relieved and happy that he too found someone, if what I was thinking was right.

***

"Idiot get up and look at what I wrote!" I went to Ayan's room and pushed him out of his bed.

"God, Aarika you are insane! Show that to me."

"Read it quickly."

"Go bring me your guitar and watch me bring your words to life." My guitar was all dusty. I hadn't held it in my hands for like more than a month. It felt really nice to just strum the stings like that and feel the beautiful melody being produced.

"You five-year-old kid! Stop playing with your guitar and give it to me. By the way, that song you wrote is for me, right? What a great person I am to make others write songs in my love and praise." If anyone ever wanted to learn self-obsession and love for oneself, then Ayan was the best teacher.

"Who said it is for you? It's for Samar," I tried to be funny and then Samar's name just slipped out of my tongue. But then I realised that Samar wasn't someone to be taken as a joke and a glower appeared on Ayan's face as well. I just didn't want to recall everything that happened. I really wished just like a computer, our brain had a delete button too. And Samar could delete his memory of falling in love with me.

"Aarika! Are you giving me that guitar or not?" He was not in a mood of joking anymore and was really serious. I wanted to ask him a thousand questions but I just didn't want to spoil his mood, his smile to fade away. I gave him the guitar and he started to sing as well.

"*Love was my vision, until they forced me to become blind*

But I had a collision when you were standing behind.

The shimmer in your eyes drew me in,

But it is your love that made me see again."

"I can't believe that you actually did it!" I couldn't believe my words being put into music so perfectly.

"I know, I know. I am great!"

The next day we went to Sony studio for the recording of our new song. The people there were really shocked to see Ayan sing so professionally without any training. They promised to sign a lot of contracts with him in future. Ayan couldn't believe his ears. I was really excited to see the public's reaction to this. I just couldn't wait!

***

Some days I wish I could go back in life. Not to change anything but just to feel a few things over and over again. It is strange how some people give you those unforgettable and beautiful moments in a few minutes which can never be given by some people, even in centuries. I didn't even realise how the time for Ayan to go back came so close. It was as if Ayan just came the previous day. That's how time passes.

A day before the wedding, Kevin invited all his close friends to our place. Many of his friends were there but I couldn't see Ayan anywhere. He never really went anywhere without telling me or for that matter without me, because he hardly knew any place in London. I was worried about his uncanny disappearance. I called him several times, left a thousand messages, but neither the messages nor the calls reached him. Maybe he had gone to Joe for some hotel related matter. Mom and dad had come too. I waited the whole night but he didn't come. It was Kevin's wedding the next day, how could he leave me alone at this moment!

***

The wedding started with singing of hymns and a few people sang solos. Even Ayan and I had planned to sing, but what followed next didn't let that happen. When I saw him entering the church, I quickly rushed to him.

"Where were you the previous night Ayan?"

"I don't see the need to tell you everything. Stop interfering in my life so much."

"What's wrong with you? Why are you talking like that? And your voice, why does it sound so different? I told you to take good care of your throat. Remember, we had to sing today?" Rather than snapping back I asked him another question politely.

"What do you think of me Aarika? Am I a kid?" Turning his eyes to the other side he spoke. He was full of rage.

"Well, if you remember we had planned to sing for Kevin's wedding. So, if you allow, shall we?" I tried really hard to control my temper.

"I am not like you whose life is just singing. I have much important things to do." His words hit me like a sword and the worst thing was that I had no idea of what was happening and why all that was happening.

"May I know what has happened to you all of a sudden?"

"As I said earlier, I don't see the need to tell you everything. So please stop questioning me and please leave me alone so that I can enjoy the wedding."

"You aren't even worth talking to Ayan. Just do whatever you want to." I had lost my temper and I simply walked away. I didn't want a person like him to destroy the essence of my brother's wedding. But deep inside I was also wondering what possibly could have gone wrong? Had his disease returned? Or someone instigated him against me? These were the only possibilities I could see, but I didn't want anything to spoil my mood or my excitement.

Candles were lit and parents were seated. The processional music began with the seating of the honoured guests. I eagerly waited for Samar. I called him a thousand times but neither did he pick up the phone nor, he came. This made me believe that he was really angry. I blew a fuse when I saw Ayan standing at the other corner of the church giving me absurd looks. The minister and Kevin entered the stage from right along with the groomsmen. Bridesmaids entered from down the centre aisle. Maid of Honour entered and after her the Flower Girl and Ring Bearer came. And finally, Rihanna entered. Wearing her white gown, Rihanna looked more charming than anyone I had seen. Kevin, in his black tuxedo and Rihanna in her glamorous gown were looking the best couple I had ever seen.

The prayer started and the congregation was seated. "Who gives this woman in marriage to this man?" The minister said. "We do," Rihanna's parents replied in unison. The worship songs started again. "Let me charge you both to remember that your future happiness is to be found in mutual consideration, patience, kindness, confidence. Kevin, it is your duty to love Rihanna as yourself, provide tender leadership and protect her from danger. Rihanna, it is your duty to treat Kevin with respect, support him, and create a healthy and happy home. You are to be undivided and one." The minister said to Kevin and Rihanna, and after that the pledge was taken, followed by the vows, and finally the exchange of rings. The guests had lunch and then they left.

The much-awaited day of my life was just... What do I call it? Ruined. The day for which I had been preparing for months passed so quickly. Ayan's behaviour wouldn't have hurt me much if I had known the reason, but he was just not ready to tell me anything. Everything was so strange. Everything was so perfect, so beautiful the night before Kevin's wedding. The same question kept troubling me. What happened in that one night that changed Ayan so much! From his way of talking to his way of walking, everything had changed completely.

2018
am I real?

After two days mom and dad went back to India and Kevin and Rihanna went for a month's vacation. Ayan was supposed to go back too, but I don't know for what reason he wasn't going.

"What the heck is this Ruby? Is this how you make food? The amount of salt you've used in these dishes could be used in seven days' food. From tomorrow onwards I am going to cook. You are fired!" Ayan said, pushing his plate away furiously.

"Excuse me? If you aren't suffering from any disorder then you should remember that the dishes you've been appreciating for a month were cooked by her only and this isn't your house. You've no right to chuck anyone out of here. Why don't you just leave? Shanaya aunty needs you." I never ever thought that I would ever say these things to Ayan but he earned it all himself. I had started to doubt my choice of marrying him.

"Did anyone talk to you? No, right? Then you better stay out of this." He held the dishes cooked and went to the kitchen.

"To hell with you Ayan!" I yelled. "And Ruby you aren't going to go anywhere."

Leaving behind everything you were long ago gone,

But today the wind of your memories has blown

I am trying hard not to cry

But laugh at the memories and not sigh.

I won't let go, cannot ever let go the hold of your memories,

You may not be with me but they'll stay with me for centuries

Losing you, wasn't losing you but every bit of me

Along with me you are also new, that I can see.

I miss those days when I used to feed you with my quandary

And you found a taste of humour in it promptly.

When you'd cry I'd wipe away all of your tears,

When you'd scream I'd fight away all of your fears,

I wish we could hold hands like we've through all of these years,

But oh, darling you seem to be nowhere near!

Love, I am trying not to make it sad

But just hoping that someday you'll come back.

You aren't with me, that is not the complaint,

But without you I am not at all insane.

By you I don't mean you who is sitting just next to me,

But my friend, who long ago with the wind flee.

It was killing me deep inside that how a person like Ayan could create so much negativity in the house. We had dinner and went to our rooms. From that day onwards, my life became so complicated that even an intelligent detective couldn't have the answers to my questions. It became like that intricate maze in which the further you go, the more you get lost. More intricate than anyone could imagine.

Day 1

I woke up with a burning sensation on my left cheek and found blood on the tips of my nails. When I got up and went in front of the mirror, I just couldn't believe my eyes. There was a big deep wound on my cheek which no one could get from their nails no matter how sharp they were, but also there wasn't anything else which I could suspect of hurting me. I thought it was just a scratch and ignored it, though it hurt badly, and went to have breakfast.

"You are still here. I wonder how shameless one could be. Have you no concern for your mother?" I said to Ayan when I saw him having food and reading the magazine as if it was his own house. But he was more shameless than I thought him to be. He didn't even care to reply. I thought to myself that I won't let his presence affect me anymore. I had my breakfast and rushed to the studio for recording my new song.

***

"How are you now Aarika?" An unknown face with spectacles on her face asked me.

"Where am I?" I was lying on the bed in some unfamiliar place. I couldn't open my eyes properly due to severe headache.

"Don't worry, you are all right now. You just collapsed. We are still not sure of the cause but some tests will be done until then, we have to keep you under watch. Your driver and friend are waiting outside, want me to call them? By the way I am Grace Weasley."

"Thank you, doctor. No, I don't feel like meeting anyone right now." I knew the friend she was talking about was Ayan, and I also knew that meeting him would only make me worse. But Ayan didn't wait for the doctor to call him, he himself entered the room.

"How is she now, doctor?" I was shocked to hear this polite tone of his again. All of a sudden, so concerned.

"She seems fine now, but still we need to do some tests to be sure. By the way Aarika, you are like a nightingale. I am a huge, huge fan of yours."

"Thanks a lot, Dr. Weasley."

"Doctor, I want to take her home. You idiot, why do you exert so much? What if something happened to you today? I know you won't feel any better if you are surrounded by the walls of hospital. Only my company can make you feel better." This just shattered my ego. I forgot all the promises I made to myself this morning and actually felt that he had again become the same good Ayan. So, I was ready to go anywhere he wanted me to. I needed the answers to my questions.

"But..." Doctor Grace was about to say something, but Ayan didn't let her complete.

"Thank you so much, Doctor. Come on Aarika." We both left without saying anything.

"You are insane Ayan. But I am glad you are back to your right senses. Now would you like to tell me what happened?" I asked him as we sat in the car.

"Let bygones be bygones Martins. Now close your eyes and don't say anything or else I will leave you in that hospital again," he said keeping his finger on my lips.

"I don't know, but I am still feeling really drowsy and my head is hurting badly."

"That's why I am telling you to close your eyes and take rest. You are just very tired after Kevin's wedding."

"Maybe you are right."

"Sleep now."

After a really long time I felt that my friend had come back, but strange things were happening to me. I was unnecessarily feeling really dizzy, agitated, and drowsy. On the other hand, I was really delighted as I could finally, after a really long time, see Ayan once again beaming a beatific smile, coupled with the unpleasantness leaving my house.

***

Day 2

I could see the sun shining as it should, Ayan enjoying the food at the dining table, my guitar in place, hearing the soft music playing in the house as it plays daily. Everything was so regular and perfectly normal, in its place. If something was out of place then it was my mind, for I couldn't recall anything happening to me. I woke up with another deep cut on my nose and felt myself become weaker than I was the previous day. It wasn't the cuts or my weakness that was troubling me, but my memory. How can a person not feel anything, be so deeply asleep that he didn't even realise getting hurt so badly? Life is strange. Your whole life you try so hard to get some things out of your mind, but you can't, and then there are moments when you try to remember that one simple thing, but you can't do that either.

"What, have you been trying to make drawings on your face with a blade?" Ayan laughed.

"Ayan, please. This isn't funny. I can't remember how I've been getting all these wounds on my face."

"Told you already, you should be in a mental hospital." He again started laughing. This was so not an Ayan thing. I still remember when I was worried about the slightest problem of my life, Ayan was even more concerned about me than myself. But I could not find a speck of that concern anywhere around him.

"Ayan run!" I yelled.

"Why?"

"Turn around."

"What?"

"Don't you see that man standing behind you? No, don't you come any closer. I'll call the police. No, get off me. Move away! Ayan, what are you doing? Why aren't you doing anything?" Shivers ran down my spine when I saw that man in the black moving towards me with a knife in his hand and Ayan not doing anything.

"Aarika, whom are you talking to? Chloe, Hazel, Felix come here." The expression on Ayan's face was such as if nothing unusual or dangerous was happening. As if there wasn't anyone standing at all.

"Yes sir?" All the servants came when Ayan called them.

"Do you guys see anyone standing here?"

"No sir."

"See Aarika? What's wrong with you?"

"No. This can't be true!" I was traumatized.

Why were all those things happening to me? I just couldn't understand anything. My brain had stopped working. I had reached that point when neither you are in a condition to think anything nor speak anything but just whimper. The whole day I didn't step out of my room. I neither picked up any one's calls, nor ate anything. I felt myself become weaker both mentally and physically.

Day 3

I woke up to the sound of someone running upstairs. I went to Ayan's room and he was sleeping. I checked the time and it was just 5 in the morning, so there was no chance for any servant to be up. So, this alarmed me to the entry of an intruder. I could still hear the sound. I was barely able to run, but I tried to walk on the highest speed as I could. But I checked every corner of the house and didn't see anyone.

"Ayan, Ayan! Wake up Ayan! There's an intruder in the house. I have been hearing the noise for so long now." My voice had become too feeble to wake up someone like him who was so deep in sleep. But I tried again. I used my same old technique of waking up people with water. I threw a small mug full of water on him.

"Are you out of your mind Aarika!" He yelled.

"Ayan, please go and check quickly. I have been hearing noises of someone running, but I can't see anyone. I am sure someone is there."

I could still hear the sound, but he could neither hear the sound nor see anyone. I had no other option rather than ignoring everything, though I felt some odd sensations inside my body. I went in front of the mirror and looked at myself. My face looked so wounded that I would be the perfect person to play the role of a ghost in a horror movie. I checked my phone and then realised that it was the big night for me. The award night. My album had been nominated. How could I miss it? But I was ashamed of going to the night full of glamour with such a face.

When Ayan woke up, I shared the problem with him. "I think you should definitely go. I'll accompany and take care of you. Don't worry." He tried his best to show that he cared for me. But when I looked into his eyes, they didn't say the same. They were not worried about me. They were not the ones that craved for me a few days back. They were least bothered about me. They didn't care if I existed or not. I finally decided that I'll go for the function. I thought that going out would help me change my mood and hopefully these strange things would stop happening to me.

Aaliya helped me get dressed up. She tried her best to conceal my wounds, but they were too fresh and dark to be concealed. I wore a short red sequined dress with my hair tied in a bun. "Aaliya, what are you doing?" I laughed as I felt as if she was tickling me really hard.

"Sorry ma'am, but I don't know what you're talking about. I was busy looking for your hair accessories," she replied, all baffled. I had realised now that there was something seriously wrong with me and I needed to see a doctor. But for the time being, I got ready for the award show. I really wished Brooke was here, I really needed her right now. But she and Flynn were on a vacation. Flynn's aunt gave them passes for Beyonce's concert in Milan. So, they were out on a vacation and I really didn't want to disturb them.

For the first time in a very long while I didn't feel confident about myself. I tried really hard to avoid the media and luckily, I was successful in doing that. Without meeting anyone I just went and sat quietly with Ayan.

"Ayan, I want to go and see a doctor tomorrow," I told Ayan while we were seated there.

"Sure darling. You are just too stressed, you need to relax for a while. Enjoy the night today," He said with a smile. Soon the award show began and they announced that I had won the award for my song 'Rendezvous'. As I was going on the stage, I saw thousands of cockroaches crawling up my legs on to my waist. "Help! Help!" I screamed, and started running here and there. As I looked up, I saw everyone with their mouths wide open. The most shocking thing was that nobody was getting up to help me. "What, are you guys insane? Can't you see these bloody cockroaches climbing up my legs! Ouch! For God's sake help me! You bloody losers, HELP ME! Arghh, my hair!" I yelled running here and there and then made a mess of my hair when the cockroaches reached there. There was a deafening silence. Some of them were trying hard to control their laughter. Why wasn't anyone doing anything! Why weren't they helping me! Where was Ayan! I stood there, with my eye makeup spreading all over my face due to my tears. And my legs and hands were bleeding. I couldn't take this anymore before everything went black and I fainted.

Day 4

As soon as I opened my eyes, I ran to see myself in the mirror. And as I expected a new scratch was there on my face, on the right cheek. I never ever thought that I could look so ugly. Four days back, everything was so normal and then within a blink of an eye everything had changed. But the scratch wasn't the only unusual thing I saw in the mirror.

"What have I done to you? What do you want from me?" I had become really weak to run or to scream and screech. Along with the whispers, tears rolled down my eyes.

"Your death." That man in the black was back. His face was covered with the hood of his sweatshirt. If anything was visible, then it was his devilish grin. He was wearing the same clothes and holding the same knife in his hand. If anything had changed about him, then it was his grin that had become more devilish. After hearing his reply, I ran back to my bed and wrapped myself in the blanket. But that didn't help. He appeared there too. My voice had become too feeble to reach out to anyone from my room. Somehow, I managed to get hold of my phone and called Ayan.

"What happened Aarika, why are you crying?"

"Look, that man, he's still there. He just told me that he wants to kill me. No! Ayan stop him! Ouch!" I just couldn't bear the sight of that man throwing bugs on my legs. It reminded me of yesterday. I began to scratch them like a lunatic in an attempt to remove them. My legs started bleeding.

"I can neither see the bugs nor the man! What are you talking about Aarika? You are still dreaming. Just sleep some more and everything will be fine."

"Why am I seeing things which no one else is seeing? Why am I feeling things which no one else is feeling? Even the mineral water tastes like poison to me. The same dishes that I used to love have now become tasteless. I can still feel those bugs all over my legs. And all those cuts? Have I unknowingly been trying to hurt myself? Why Ayan? WHY? Why do I feel there's no life left in me?" Wiping my tears, I again lay in my bed trying to figure out the answers to my questions.

"You know who does these things? Mentally disabled people," I couldn't figure out if he was joking or making me aware of what I had become. But whatever it was I had become too weak to fight back.

"Please call the doctor Ayan," I cried in an almost inaudible voice.

"Aarika, it's six in the morning. Shut up and go to sleep."

Weeping, I didn't even realise when I fell asleep. I was awakened by a weird sound and then I saw a toy come into my room yelling in a spooky, cacophonous voice:

"Jack and Jill went up the hill

To fetch a pail of water,

Jack fell down and broke his crown,

And Jill came tumbling after."

I didn't even know if it was real or not. I had no energy left in me to react. It was high time now. I decided to call the doctor myself, but neither Ayan was there nor my phone. I couldn't exactly remember what happened yesterday, but as I went and asked Ayan, whatever he told me was so horrifying that I was too scared to face the world now. That was going to be all over the news now. I couldn't even gather my nerves to turn on the television or check my phone. I didn't know what to do. But I knew that I was a joke for the entire world right now, and the media had finally got its hot gossip. I knew the new world that I would enter into would be much different from the world I had left behind. In this new world I would have lost all my dignity.

How was all this happening to me even possible? I didn't know where to go! Throughout the day I heard voices, felt things, and saw things, which no one else could see or no one else could feel. I had started feeling afraid of my own face, started fearing my own hands for I didn't know when they would start hurting my own body.

However, by evening I finally saw a doctor entering. She examined me but she couldn't see anything wrong with me. Still, she prescribed some medicines which would calm my mind and help me feel better. After I ate dinner, Ayan came and gave me the medicine.

Day 5

As I woke up, I saw that man sitting just next to me with a lighter in his hand.

"There's petrol all over the floor of your room," he told me with a devilish grin, deliberately showing me the lighter to scare me.

"Ruby! Come here!"

"Yes ma'am?

"Please take away this lighter from his hands or else he is going to burn the house," I yelled, frantically trying to get up from my bed.

"Take the lighter from whom Madam?" she asked, all baffled.

"Ruby, don't you see this man sitting just next to me?" I had been thinking all that while that Ayan and everyone were seeing everything, but just playing some pranks with me. But when even Ruby refused to see those things, I was perplexed. I really trusted Ruby and she couldn't lie.

"Sorry, but to be honest I don't see anyo…"

"Run Ruby! Do something!" I screamed for help when I saw him throwing the lit lighter and the fire being ignited.

"Ma'am, relax. There's no one here." Ruby came and hugged me.

I knew why all this was happening to me. You see I had reached the imbecile stage of relating every bad thing that I had done in my life to every bad thing that was happening to me in the present. I really did bad to Samar and the same was happening to me now. I needed to see him. I needed to see him at any cost! I needed to fall down on my knees and apologize to him. My selfishness had made my life hell like.

"Come on Ruby, help me dress up and reach the car, and then we'll go to see another doctor." I found myself regaining some energy. I didn't want to waste even a single minute and finally got up from my bed after ages with the help of my stick. That is the reason I fear old age so much. It makes you feel that whatever you have within you has become useless and you are just a piece of waste lying in one corner of the house, even unable to move without someone's help. But little did I know that I would have to face this feeling at such a young age. But that day I had to fight it all. I had to apologise for my mistakes. I should have told Samar the very day I realised that I love Ayan. I shouldn't have neglected him this way. I shouldn't have broken his heart. I was too eager now to correct my mistakes.

When I reached Samar's place, I rang the doorbell several times but no one opened the door. That reminded me of the keys Samar gave me and I entered the house with their help. But as I went inside I felt myself getting fits of giddiness again due to the smell. I had never come across anything more malodorous than his house. I didn't even know if that smell was for real, because I had been coming across such things lately but not as fetid as that.

I followed the smell and felt it increase near Samar's room. I didn't know why as I was moving towards his room, my heart started beating faster. It was like an intuition of something bad. But the room was locked. So, I tried to unlock it with the keys Samar gave me and fortuitously it opened. I was shaken to see so many paintings of myself in his room. They were painted very beautifully, but now they were torn. Maybe that was a big sign of how much Samar had begun to hate me. On some paintings it was even written 'Die Aarika'. I couldn't help but cry. Maybe the hatred he had for me now was much fierce than the love he had for me once. But to find the cause of the smell I checked the drawers, looked beneath the bed, looked inside the bathroom too. But I couldn't find anything. The only place left was Samar's cupboard.

I nearly jumped out of my skin when I opened the cupboard. I could see a hand coming out from a pile of clothes. The watch seemed very familiar to me. I removed the clothes and what I saw next made my heart beat stop. I told myself that I was hallucinating again. This is what I had been doing for days. Seeing things which never existed and causing trouble not only to myself, but everyone around me.

No, this could not be true. There was no way this could have happened. There should have never been a place for a person like me among the normal people, but I should have been in a mental asylum. How was it possible that the dead body was of Ayan? I saw him sleeping myself not fifteen minutes ago. No. There wasn't any chance for him to be dead. NO! The dead body smelled like it had been rotting for more than a week.

"Ruby!" I ran down, rushing to Ruby who was sitting in the car. "Ruby, come quickly with me."

"Madam you don't look okay, shouldn't we go to the doctor first?"

"No! You just come with me!" I felt as if rather than of skin, my body had become of sweat.

"Okay, but please be calm or else it may make you worse."

"Just tell me that you don't smell anything strange here." Keeping my fingers crossed, for the first time in a while I actually wished that I was hallucinating.

"No madam I do. This place is argh so putrid!"

"No! No this can't be true! Come upstairs with me!"

"Madam I can't withstand this smell, let's just get out of here."

"Please tell me that you don't see anything strange in this cupboard?" Ruby froze with fear. Minutes passed, but she didn't utter a single word.

"Ruby please say something!" She broke into tears. That was enough to tell me that what I saw wasn't a delusion.

IT WAS AYAN! There was a knife stabbed right in his chest. His head had been half shaved. His face was badly hurt. His hands were freezing, and his skin had become purplish pink. His clothes were all red with blood. He was in such a bad condition that it would have been really difficult for me to recognize him had it not been for the shoes and the wrist watch that he bought with me. Ruby couldn't stop crying. And I, I just sat there with his hands in mine. Shock robbed me of speech. How could the hands that once gave me so much comfort become all wretched? How could the one who was so full of life lie lifeless?

"How could you do this to me Ayan? What about all those promises of never leaving each other, of releasing a thousand albums? Why did you come back again when you had to leave me? Who'll take care of me? Who'll dance with me like that? Who'll wake me up when I am just about to fall asleep? Why did you do it?" I lamented to his dead body. I felt the whole world collapsing upon me. Tears began rolling down my cheeks like rivulets. The pain that I felt at the thought of becoming mad was so immense that I can't even express it in words. But this was even worse than that. But if I delayed for one minute more than maybe I would lose my chance to get justice for Ayan. Just when I was about get up, I heard the floor creaking, and I froze with fear as I saw him.

"*Jack and Jill went up the hill*

To fetch a pail of water,

Jack fell down and broke his crown,

And Jill came tumbling after.

Jack is dead, and Jill will die after

Hello Jill, uh I mean Aarika." It was Samar. He greeted me with an evil grin and opened his arms to hug me.

"Ruby, it would be really great if you could excuse us for some time. You and David wait in the car. It won't take me long." I knew Samar was definitely up to something and I didn't want Ruby to get into any of this because of me. I definitely knew that it was Samar who killed Ayan, I just wanted to know how and why. I knew when Samar said he'll kill me if I showed up ever again, that he actually meant it.

"Ok ma'am." Ruby wiped her tears and started moving.

"Wait, Ruby. You can wait in Aunt Lara's room, she won't be home for at least a month more. And give that phone to me."

Samar grabbed Ruby's hand and pushed her into Aunt Lara's room. Just when he was busy in locking the room, I tried to run out of the house to save mine and Ruby's life. But that's when I felt my hair being pulled tightly. Samar grabbed my hair and dragged me to his room.

"You bitch! I won't let you escape! Not this time." He kept holding my hair in his hand and pushed me down on to the floor. My head banged against the wall and I felt faintish.

"Why did you kill him? Why, Samar! Tell me, why?" I asked with bloodshot eyes.

"What's the hurry baby? I am meeting you after so long, let me shower some love upon my darling fiancé. Oh fiancé? Bloody fiancé!" He picked me up from my arm and threw me on a chair. He opened his drawer and brought a rope.

"This rope, is the same one with which I tied your beloved. And then..." He tied me to the chair with the help of the rope and began laughing like a true lunatic. "And then I murdered him!" His laughter became even louder.

"But why and how did you do it!" I screamed as loudly as possible.

"Close your eyes," He said, looking for something in the bag he brought along with him this morning.

"Samar, stop playing games now and tell me everything!"

"I said close your eyes!" He shouted at me and put a knife around my neck.

"You are hurting me Samar," I said, crying and closing my eyes.

"As if I care. Open them now!" I couldn't believe my eyes. I was all baffled. I felt as it was not Samar but Ayan standing in front of me. His same chuck hazel eyes, his same sharp pointed nose. Everything was just like Ayan's.

"How did you do it!" He started unbuttoning the shirt and from a little below the neck removed the real flesh mask and lenses from his eyes. I didn't even know if it was actually possible to make such masks. I was sure, even the most brutal murderer on this earth wouldn't have been able to think that far. Real flesh mask! Oh, good God.

"You are evil, you are so evil Samar! Why did you do it? Why!"

"If you scream once more you can't even imagine what I'll do to you. Just shut that stupid mouth of yours. And you want to know why, then listen. First, Ayan was my beloved younger brother" Samar said.

Now all their similarities, everything started making sense to me. But still infinite questions were flooding in my mind.

"Second, I am a psychopath." It felt as if one by one all my organs had stopped functioning. Slowly he was shooting me with such bitter truths that were way too much for me to handle. But the truth that wounded my heart the most was that despite killing his own brother, how could he be so normal, absolutely without any guilt?

"My family was the perfect family. The happy family that they have in books and movies. Our day wasn't complete if Ayan and I didn't talk and laugh with each other. We weren't two separate people. We were one. We used to paint together, play so much with each other. But that was only until we were kids. When we got to know that dad had Huntington's chorea, our tests were done too. Ayan had it but luckily, I didn't. From that day onwards, my life changed. Before that day I had felt that I was the naughtiest yet the most pampered in the house, but that day the bubble of my dream burst and I started feeling that my worth in the house was no more than a statue. Nobody had the time to talk to me. If anybody cared about anyone in the house, then it was for Ayan. Out of frustration I started harming Ayan. And that's how my lovely family contributed in the making of a psychopath. The most dangerous psychopath. I began by killing my first pet, Tucker. Then I was unstoppable.

Ah, I hate those people so much. Mom couldn't tolerate this and decided to send me to live with my uncle. Vikrant uncle and Aunt Lara looked after me as if I was their own child. The care, the love that I always looked for at my home, I found it in their house within a few days. Everything started to become normal but as days passed the hatred for mom, dad and Ayan became more and more and I refused to meet any of them. They came to meet me several times, called up several times but I wasn't ready to even look at their faces. I tried, I tried a lot, went to rehab, oh God, I don't even want to recall those days, and then finally with my Aunt and Uncle's support I started to become normal. I still couldn't be absolutely normal. When I had the urge to harm anyone, it's me who I chose. Thus, the wounds on my face and hand. And when I found you, for the first time in my life I felt that I was happy, satisfied. I was always bored, but never of you." He spoke running his fingers through my uncombed hair and slowly running the knife up and down through my body. He was roaring with laughter and had the same twinkle in his eyes that a lion has when he finally finds his prey.

"You were so beautiful, specially your heart, that I wanted to tear it down into a hundred pieces. I mean that on a literal way, by the way. You were irresistible, so irresistible to hurt, to torture, to play with. But thanks to Ayan! Just like he took away mom and dad, he wanted to take away you too. How could I let him do that? If he would take you away, whom would I hurt? Whom would I play with? When you both were having that delicious breakfast, I was there. When you both were dancing so merrily, I was watching you both. I watched Ayan, his body language, his pickup lines, God, they were damn good. The way you used to blush when he called you Martins, I saw each and every bloody small thing. But when you said that you love Ayan, I just couldn't control myself and wanted to kill you both right away. I felt… I felt betrayed. You bloody cheater! But that would make me land in trouble. So, with a lot of planning I killed that bastard. He is the first human that I ever killed. And now that I have started, I won't stop. The next is going to be Flynn, wasn't he the one who corrupted your mind? Oh and, I killed Alyssa too. She is a cheater too, cheated on her ex-boyfriend to be with me. She is right there in the next room." He started laughing and rotating his head again. It was like that moment was the happiest one of his life. I was wearing many layers of wool, yet my hands were freezing. I was hardly able to speak, but I tried to scream as much as I could at that point of time.

"How the hell can you kill your own brother!" I had become so weak that I was barely able to open my eyes. That pain, that anger, all of it was ineffable.

"And oh, wait, how can I not tell you HOW I killed my beloved brother? Like a very caring and angel like brother I called him up a day before Kevin's wedding and told him how sorry I was for what all I did, how much I had missed him and everyone all that while, and how badly I wanted to make things all right between us and wanted to cherish each and every moment of life with him. His happiness knew no bounds and he came running to my place like anything. Aunt Lara had gone to Scotland to take care of her ill mother and uncle was out on a business tour to Chicago. I knew both of them wouldn't return before a month or two, so it was a brilliant opportunity for me. Ayan had almost believed the fact that I seriously wanted to make things all right with him.

He was relishing the lavish dinner and reminiscing hilarious incidents from childhood and that was when I...I hit him with a flower vase on his head to make him unconscious. Then I dragged him and tied him to the chair that you are tied to right now and gave him shocks and tortured him. Then I started destroying his beauty that you…you loved so much. I even shaved half his head and then last of all stabbed him in the chest. A thousand times I stabbed him until his painful screams vanished and then I hid his body in the cupboard. I wanted to bury both your bodies together. I had already made all the arrangements of real flesh mask, lenses, got my hair cut just like him. You were the one who was always saying that I looked like him, so I took its advantage. Oh, how good that day was! The best and most beautiful day of my life."

"How can your eyes adore the sight of your own brother's blood? What are you? A human can't be like this. Wait! Do you have any hand in what all is happening to me?"

"Oh yes, yes my darling! How…how could I let a bitch like you go so easily? Each night I would mix some medicines in your food which made you sleepy and hallucinate things. That's why I wanted to take charge of cooking and fired Ruby. Sometimes it was your imagination that haunted you, sometimes it was me. That man in the black was your hallucination, but that toy was real. I hated you even more than Ayan, maybe because I had started loving you the most or maybe you never let me get bored. I had to keep you away from me so that you didn't suspect anything, only then I could accomplish my mission of killing you as well. I couldn't afford to let you see me much. No…no I had to kill you at any cost. And I will kill you for sure. Each night I would come to your room and try to kill you but something stopped me. So, I decided to let you only kill yourself. I would enjoy watching that more. I would love to see you get all frustrated just the way you frustrated me. I wanted you to become so insane that one day you could even kill yourself. I wanted you to Goddamn hate yourself and die! I wanted you to hang yourself to death. I wished that your heart broke in as many pieces as you broke mine. But you were a fighter and were destined to be killed by me. And, I will kill you soon, baby." He started laughing even more loudly.

"Stop it Samar! I don't want to hear you anymore!" He has ruined me. My life, my career, everything. Ayan was my best friend, my life, the one who actually taught me what the true meaning of life was. Ayan never expected to live any longer than this, but little did he know that his disease won't be the reason of his death but his own brother. Samar didn't murder only Ayan, but everyone who knew him, for anyone who knew him couldn't stop themselves from loving him. I always used to think that I had seen Samar at his worst, I had tasted all his darkness, but now I know sometimes there exists even a darker side to the dark.

It had almost been eight hours since I had been stuck at Samar's house. He was neither killing me nor letting me go. He'd just been laughing like lunatics without even uttering a single word. And I, I felt as if someone was pricking a needle right in my heart. I wanted to go and seek justice for my love, but there was no way out. My love's dead body was lying right in front of me, he had in fact pushed it so close to my feet now. It was hard to even breathe in that room.

"Why don't you kill me, Samar! What are you waiting for?" I was way too curious to know why he had kept me alive till then.

"Why? Being alive hurts too much now, doesn't it? What about you and your darling's theories about being full of life, feeling alive and making each moment count? They have flown away, right? Oh, what a demon! What a good demon I am." Samar was not in his right senses. He had totally lost his mind.

"Tomorrow, 15th December. 15th December is the date I am waiting for."

"What's so special about that?" I asked.

"That is the first time I met you. The very day when my eyes met yours and then were head over heels in love with them. That was the first time I felt butterflies flying in my stomach, locked my door and danced like anything. You made me feel things. Or maybe my brain found a way to kill my boredom. Argh! Those bloody memories! But I don't want these to be the memories for that day. From now on, the only memory of this day will be your dead body, your rotten ugly face, crying and begging for help." After he said that, just one question popped up in my mind, *How can someone be so insane*? This guy had crossed all the limits of insanity. I had lost all hopes of escaping. But then I heard someone ring the bell, which, for a change finally made Samar's laughter stop. He looked down through the window and quickly untied my ropes and pushed Ayan's body back into the cupboard.

"If you utter a single word bitch, you are dead. If anyone asks you anything just tell them you came here to meet me. Oh crap! If you love your life be normal. Absolutely normal." It was the police. Behind them, I saw David standing. I couldn't believe that he could be this wise. There was no way for Samar to escape now. I yelled as loudly as I could and tried to drag myself out of the chair to go downstairs and open the door. But it was all futile. Samar was holding me by my hair, strongly. But I saw the knife that Samar had dropped when he got all panicky. I grabbed it with the help of my foot and losing no time I hurt Samar with it on his leg. He let go of my hair and held his leg. It pained my heart so much to just give him a few cuts on his leg, I wonder how without any guilt he killed two people with it. I reached downstairs, with a lot of difficulty.

"Officer, there's a dead body inside that room!" I told them each and everything and rescued Ruby. God knows what would've happened if David didn't reach in time.

"How did you know, David?" I asked him curiously, still unable to figure how he got to know.

"I waited long after you and Ruby went inside. I didn't want to leave you alone, I was worried about you. That was when I saw him laughing madly with his evil laughter. I knew then that your lives were in danger. I informed the police and the rest you know."

"Thanks a lot David, and please inform Kevin. I know this will ruin their holiday, but I know he wouldn't want to miss a chance to say good bye to him one last time. Ruby, I am so sorry you got into all this because of me." I spoke crying loudly and hugging David and Ruby.

Samar was sentenced to life imprisonment and I was taken to the hospital immediately. I couldn't sleep for nights. Each time I closed my eyes his face would come in front of me. Even the flowers, the trees mourned his death. It was as if there were no stars in the sky, only dark clouds. I learned much more from Ayan than from anyone else. He taught me to sing. He taught me about this universe. He taught me to laugh, live and love and most importantly the true meaning of happiness. I couldn't even pick my phone to tell Shanaya aunty about all this. None of us would have felt the pain that Shanaya aunty would have.

Some days I feel bad for Samar too. Had he received medical help and some support, none of us would have faced what we are facing today. Mental illnesses are more serious and much scarier than anyone of us know and should be treated as soon as symptoms start showing up.

Epilogue

"No matter how far from me takes you death,

You'll be alive in my each and every breath."

The thing that hurts me the most is that Ayan wasn't alive to see his own success. Our song was finally released and people found it my best work till date. I had plans to live with Ayan forever, but didn't know that I'll not even get to live with him for a complete year. Samar committed suicide in the jail after five months.

Now that you aren't around

Not much can I see that's changed.

I inhale, I exhale, my legs work just fine,

My smile is the same, my face is still mine.

The flowers are blooming, the trees are growing,

The day is falling and the stars are glowing.

The only trouble in my nights is my sleep,

Each night the sleeping pills compete with the fading memory of your voice so deep.

And your slender fingers caressing my hair,

Oh, this competition is just so unfair!

The comfort of your lap still haunts,

These pills do sing but a cacophonous song.

And every night they lose this competition,

They just give me an uneasy sleep

From the dark ebony sky, shining among thousands of stars

I wish you could come and lull me to a beautiful sleep.

My story taught me one thing: Life is very uncertain. One moment is full of life, the next maybe lifeless. Such is life's uncertainty. We just have to make every moment count because we don't know what may come next. I had to do a great deal of hard work for explaining everything and making my career again. I can't thank Brooklyn and Flynn enough for the unconditional support they gave me. And oh, they got married and have a gorgeous daughter. Even Kevin and Rihanna never stayed back in showering their love. I was dying each day missing Ayan until I went to his house and read something written in his diary:

"I may not be with you,

But keep my memories, my thoughts and my soul with you.

Till the time they'll be with you, there'll be life in me and that way I'll never die but always live in you." — A note to everyone who loves me.

He had also written special notes for his friends and family. In my note I found this written:

For Martins

"Hey Martins, what's it like in your city? I don't know if you'll ever get to read this but if you do then I want you to know that just one word perfectly describes you. Beautiful. Not talking about your monkey face, but your heart. Every minute of those four years was the best of my life. So good that I finally don't regret dying because you've given me so many good memories in those four years which I couldn't have gotten in my whole life. And yes, I never told you this, but you actually taught me the importance of dreams. If four years have given me this, I wonder what say, ten, twenty or thirty years would have given me. But time, time is the only thing I don't have now. Two months, two weeks, two hours or two minutes, I don't know how much time I have, but I demand at least the time to complete this letter. The only regret will be that you'll not be by my side when I die. However, I feel I am lucky to die so young for how many people exactly get a chance to leave a beautiful corpse behind.

God, I can actually imagine you making that seal like noise as you cry when you read this. But now time to make some promises.

Promise me come what may, you'll not stop loving yourself. Ah, I wish I wasn't dying so early, but we can't fight death. So, I leave the rest of my dreams for you to live. I think that after me you are the craziest person on this earth so, I don't think anyone can do this job better than you. You have a fearlessness buried inside you. Promise me that you'll not leave a single nook of this world and leave a mark everywhere. Promise me that you'll make each minute count, pamper yourself as much as possible. Promise me that you'll never let that beautiful smile of yours vanish, you'll fly with the birds, swim with the fishes, jump from the highest point, experience every possible adventure and not stop dancing like insane people.

Go, wear those favourite loose striped pyjamas of yours and walk with pride. AND, AND LOVE LIFE LIKE I LOVED IT. Only then I would feel that all my dreams have been lived fully. Besides, with this letter I have attached a more systematic list of the tasks to be accomplished by you. I'll be the star that will shine the brightest in the sky and keep an eye on you, so no scope for cheating. But you, you have no right to think of me too often because that is definitely going to violate one or the other of your promises. Live well, Martins. Just live fully.

Side note: Never told you this, but I think I've fallen in love with you. Yes, you, who has a face like Shrek.

Don't lose the CD in the envelope. I have recorded your favourite song in my voice.

Love, your monkey."

He must have written at the time of his disease. I feel death is destined even before we are born. I finally understood that it doesn't matter how much we live. The only thing that matters is how much we live in those days...

Now that his tale has been told, his soul can rest in peace and I can die peacefully. With Ayan's weird letter and weird promises in it, I lived a more beautiful life than anyone could ever imagine. As I always dreamt of, to fulfil his promises I almost travelled the whole world. And guess what? As a part of those promises I got married too. His name is Matt Evens, my fellow singer and present best friend. He is at least half crazy as Ayan. And without him it would have been really difficult to fulfil all of Ayan's promises. After all these long years I can die without breaking any promise and live forever with the perfect imperfections of my life. It took me sixty-four long years to do that, but I am proud that I did it. I am sure he'll also be proud of me.

I am right now at the Sea of Stars, Maldives. Slowly stepping in the arms of the beautiful sea. Slowly letting myself drown in its loving arms. Slowly letting my eyes close and then finally opening them in his arms. I see him. I finally see him after ages. His spirit's smile is wider than ever. His eyes twinkling with joy. This sweet little world is ours now. Just me and Ayan. No rules, no limits. No contracts, no lies. Just the two of us. "Hey Martins, welcome!" he says.

THE END